# Jamhuri, Njambi
# &
# Fighting Zombies

By
Ted Neill

Dedicated to
Nnedi Okorafor, N.K. Jemisin,
& Tomi Adeyemi

Because I am but a tourist in a world where you
are the trailblazers.

# A Note on Cultural (Mis)appropriation

I have not stayed in my lane, and my sense of social justice—not to mention my friends who identify as people of color—have called me out for it. Rightly so.

At first glance, most readers might not see the trouble with a cisgender, heterosexual, white writer using imagery from African culture in a work of fiction. It's a "celebration of African traditions ignored by sci-fi and fantasy writers for far too long," or it's "an overdue acknowledgement of rich African contributions to art and literature." Maybe it's even "a healthy, contemporary reaction to the overemphasis of white characters in sci-fi and fantasy."

It is, I hope, but it's other things too—things that must be viewed in the context of colonialism and the social, political, economic, and military oppression of people of color.

First of all, I'm no trailblazer. Other writers, such as Nnedi Okorafor and N.K. Jemisin, have been producing works that fuse sci-fi and fantasy with African themes for some time. Before them, Octavia Butler was doing the same. Acknowledging, celebrating, and profiting from a white male's derivations from the art and images of people of color over those artists of color who have a more personal, historical claim is nothing new. It's a long tradition, characterizing the careers of artists as diverse as Al Jolson, Elvis Presley, The Rolling Stones, Robin Thicke, Justin Timberlake, and so many others.[1]

So, depending on the interpretation, *Jamhuri, Njambi & Fighting Zombies* is a celebration, an acknowledgement, or it's just another form of exploitation and cultural (mis)appropriation.

Truth is, it's all these things.

To simply see this work as a welcome and timely celebration, a "generous inclusion," would be to patronize these traditions and ignore great artists of color. It also ignores the historical power imbalances that have benefited Western, white writers over communities of color, whether in Africa or in its diaspora, for hundreds of years. This has been due to quirks of geography, disease, and more insidious institutions and practices such as colonialism, white supremacy, and slavery (to name just a few). Blood, treasure, images, and ideas have been extracted from these communities for centuries, the benefits accruing to whites and the cost borne by people of color. It is a repeating pattern, called out with smoldering eloquence by Jesse Williams in his acceptance speech for the 2016 Black Entertainment Television Humanitarian Award:

*This invention called whiteness uses and abuses us . . . extracting our culture, our dollars, our entertainment like oil—black gold—ghettoizing and*

---

[1] This even happens in social activism. One need look no further than the initial confusion about the origin of the "MeToo" campaign. Many Twitter followers attributed it to Alyssa Milano, when it was actually a campaign started in 2007 by Tarana Burke, a Harlem activist, as a way to support women and girls and women of color who had been victims of sexual abuse.

*demeaning our creations and stealing them,*
*gentrifying our genius and then trying us on like*
*costumes before discarding our bodies like rinds of*
*strange fruit.*

There is nothing to add to Mr. William's words. They are complete, powerful, and persuasive on their own.

There *is* a counter argument. It goes something like this: that the cross-fertilization of cultures has always taken place and led to benefits in a variety of disciplines. The very characters these words are written with are "Roman," influenced by Greek and Phoenician alphabets; the numbers in this text are "Arabic," although really first codified by a Persian scholar (Muhammad al-Khwarizmi) who modeled them after a number system used by Hindu mathematicians.

Cross-fertilization indeed.

The precedents for cultural exchange in fantasy literature are many fold. Take J.R.R. Tolkien, who borrowed heavily from Norse, Finnish, Germanic, as well as his own Anglo-Saxon traditions. Such fusions can create works of profound beauty and stand testament to the value of cultural diffusion. And it is often artists who are pioneers in reaching across cultural and social barriers, drawn by the universal experience of art and the appreciation of beauty. In the process we may blend influences, foster collaboration, and forge lifelong friendships despite ethnic, racial, or other social barriers. Sometimes amazing art is produced too.

But it is equally important to point out that Tolkien's ancestors did not systematically oppress these other groups. Furthermore, Tolkien, in his own time, did not benefit disproportionately from historic or current oppression of Scandinavians or Germanic people in a way that denied these groups equal opportunity to flourish. The exchange of trade, ideas, and even violence among these peoples took place (more or less) among groups with equivalent levels of power—on an even playing field, if you will. The costs and benefits were equally shared.

No such moral or ethical neutrality can be ascribed to the exploitation of people of color by Europeans or their white descendants. White privilege is real. It has benefited me and *still* benefits me as a white man, a white writer, in the United States.

There is no getting around this. But just because something *looks* like an unethical pattern in the past, does not mean it is the exact same thing today. In my heart of hearts, I would hope that *Jamhuri, Njambi & Fighting Zombies* is not exploitive. But intentions do not exculpate the artist. The art and work will stand for themselves and will rise or fall on the interpretation, opinions, the praise or condemnation, of others. I expect both and I have no answer other than my work.

So why write *Jamhuri, Njambi & Fighting Zombies?* Can we escape these patterns of oppression, exploitation, and historical amnesia?

I hope so.

Those who are not seized by the urge to create, to channel some idea from the world of the imagined to the real, might not understand the fierce insistence of an idea, a plot, or characters and their stories knocking around in an author's head. Like the Greek muses, these imagined personalities and events seem to exist outside us, using the artist as a mere channel. Michelangelo described it best when he said the figures he sculpted had always already existed, trapped inside their blocks of marble. It was simply his role to chip away the excess to reveal them.

It is the same with the characters and stories that reside in a writer's head. They feel, to us, as if they already do and have always existed—a bit like a law in physics, a pattern in number theory, or an undiscovered prime. We as artists reveal; we create, because we can't *not*. These characters, Jamhuri, Njambi, Latia, Anastasia, Esmeralda, and their stories, although not completely aligned with my own background, wanted to be out in the world. They wouldn't leave me alone until they were.

The second reason was a personal promise. These stories were conceived in the early 2000s when I was living and working at an orphanage for HIV+ children in Nairobi, Kenya. At the time our resources for books were limited. Although we benefited from donations, the books I read to the kids had few characters that looked like them. As much as they enjoyed Dav Pilkey's *Captain Underpants* (which did include a main character of color), they clamored for more characters that looked like them, characters from backgrounds and contexts they could relate to. As children who had been abandoned, abused, stigmatized, and generally not "seen" as individuals outside of their HIV status, this broke my heart.

At the time, writers such as Nnedi Okorafor and N.K. Jemisin were not on my own radar. So I set out to write a few stories of my own.

As a result, *Jamhuri, Njambi & Fighting Zombies* is laden with that personal history and meaning for me. If these stories never find an audience beyond the children I wrote them for, then I am at peace with that. The audience and stories deserve at least that much, if nothing else.

But this all begs the question of whether a privileged, white, male writer *can* or even *should* write from the point of view of characters of color. The answer leads me to my third and final reason for writing and publishing these stories.

"*Can* a privileged, white, male writer write from the point of view of characters of color?" I will leave that for the readers to determine. I'd like to think these characters are authentic and well developed, but sales, comment sections, and reviews will bear that out as true or not.

The question of *should* I have even tried to write in the point of view of these characters also looms large for me. I, for one, believe that art can transcend race (in *some* ways). As mentioned above, the common ground, the shared experience of being an artist, has united people from various backgrounds for the entire story of humankind. Moving from literature to music, I landed on the career and life of Benny Goodman as an example. Contemporary critics may be split over the legacy of figures such as Goodman, whose classical background and European ancestry "legitimized" jazz for white listeners, making jazz "safe" to bring into venues such as Carnegie Hall. His integration and promotion of this African American art form in his own performances undeniably contributed to his own stardom and the success of his career at a time when black musicians couldn't drink from the same water fountains, much less perform in the same concert halls as he. So in that sense, perhaps Goodman's choices were exploitive. But Goodman also launched the careers of many African American jazz artists and, during a time of racial segregation, defiantly toured the US in an integrated jazz band.

So, as they say on Facebook, the relationship status here is "complicated."

And that still does not answer the question of whether a white person *can* even write believable black characters?

It is not as straight forward as I once thought. For instance, my friends—writers of color in literature, television, and film—have had to write white characters throughout the course of their careers. It's the reality of whiteness being associated with the mainstream, with "normality." This is a consequence of our ridiculous default culture of white-centeredness and the unfortunate reality of the marketplace. The question of whether or not my friends of color "can" write white characters rarely comes up for them. After all, as people of color in the United States, they are bombarded with images of whiteness. They are forced (sadly) to move in a sea of pallor that is, arbitrarily, considered "the norm." As people of color in a predominantly white society, they *have* to understand white culture—even better than we might understand ourselves (as James Baldwin once pointed out).

Whites do not have the same need. As Jesse Williams reminds us, white society might extract black culture, treating it as a costume to put on, or a thing to demean, to make the "other." But we have the choice. If we whites wanted, we could likely pass the day without encountering a person of color IRL (in real life). With effort, (and sometimes without) we can whitewash our social experiences and our media consumption, eliminating diverse images and voices and validating only our own. Living a life in an echo chamber like this, as so many white Americans do, eliminates the need to appreciate the perspective or point of view of someone different. It is a great loss, but it happens. I know this from teaching classes on race and reconciliation to white participants. One woman in her fifties in one of my classes recently had the epiphany that, "I worked as a trauma nurse in for thirty-two years and it's dawning on me that I never worked with a black nurse. It didn't even *occur* to me that that was even remarkable until 2017."

Baldwin has written that people of color are forced to "get" us whites, to understand us. Sometimes reading white people, living in a state of double consciousness (knowing yourself but also imagining how others *misperceive* your identity), is a matter of life or death. The tragic deaths of Philando Castile, Eric Garner, Alton

Sterling, Charleena Lyles, and the murder of so many other black citizens by police can attest to this.

But to say that whites *cannot* do the same, that a white writer *cannot* and *should not* write from the point of view of black characters (as I have been told) is a conclusion I am unwilling to accept. Such a conclusion is flawed; it posits that we whites can *never* understand, much less endorse, the perspective of anyone but ourselves, even with effort, intentionality, and exposure. If this were true, it leaves me without hope. If understanding could only go in one direction: people of color learning to interpret and live with white people who are unable to do the same, progress would be impossible.

I don't want to live in that world.

It may take intentionality and no small amount of effort, humility, and discomfort, but I want—*I need*—to believe that members of a group of people who have been oppressors and a (rapidly diminishing) majority can come to understand and endorse, to love and accept the perspective of an oppressed minority. Perhaps it is the part of writers and artists, who try to see out of the eyes of others, to play a constructive role here. Again, to say otherwise—that artists, or even people in general, cannot do so—would be to suggest that people of color alone have this ability and whites do not. This seems like an overgeneralization, a dangerous assumption—in short, pure fallacy.

So yes, I believe that a white, privileged writer *can* and even *should* try to write from the perspective of others—with care, humility, and historical sensitivity. Must we be aware of harmful cultural legacies? Absolutely. We should also take care to consider whether or not our voices are taking up space that could be granted to writers of color who have not had the same opportunities to speak or to publish. The realities of the marketplace and the attention span of the modern human dictate that this is a genuine possibility. But to stop short of trying because of these risks handicaps us all.

The default flow of information, attention, experiences, and imagery might be in the direction of white people like myself—*we* the loud, obnoxious, blundering, self-absorbed, self-centered sibling of the US family, we who have historically been the referent. Thanks to demographics, this will not always be the case. But in the meantime, with intentionality, I believe this myopic vision amongst *wypipo* can be remedied. It takes exposure, dialogue, travel, reading, watching, and most of all, *shutting up and listening.*

In that spirit, I think that is enough from me. People who look like me have had the spotlight on them and the microphone clutched in their hands a long time. Acknowledging that requires me to step aside, to let the characters take the stage—in this case Jamhuri, Latia, Njambi, Anastasia, and Esmeralda, who all have their own real-life counterparts—so they might tell their stories. I'll be off to the side, sitting down and shutting up.

Thanks for reading. Hope you enjoy. If you don't, well, I'll try to do better next time.

—Ted Neill, Seattle, 2018

# ~ Prelude ~
# Falling

The first drop was the longest. Anastasia struck the first ledge with such force that it made her cry out as the air was crushed right out of her lungs. She tumbled further, her arms flung out like a dervish, the world a blur, but among the rocks, the white sky, the dust, and flashes of blood, she caught sight of the Devourer descending after her, barreling down the hillside in an avalanche of pebbles and stones. He was a hunter who had caught the scent of his prey and he was not about to let her slip away.

The slope became less sheer, but still Anastasia tumbled down, bouncing off the hillside, each turn feeling like a punch or a kick, to the face, the gut, wherever. When her momentum had run out and she was weak with the pain of the impacts and sick from the disorientation of such violent spinning, she continued to crawl forward, the noise of the Devourer closing in on her with all the clamor of an earthquake. Her only thought was to lead the nameless thing as far from her brother and all the others as possible. There were copious drops of blood on the ground from her head. Her hands were shredded and raw, the flesh scraped off, leaving bloody prints behind her. Even though she was no longer spinning, her vision was blurred. A ravine, its floor lost in shadow, loomed up to her right. Behind her she could hear the nameless thing, his claws sweeping up the bloody dirt she left behind into his mouth, his fangs crushing the stones that came along with it.

Anastasia rolled closer to the edge, hoping that she might lure him over the side, even if she had to go with him. She kept as close to the edge as possible without falling. The sides were steep and a blanket of aether fog floated in a dense layer. The Devourer moved closer, his cry of many voices like a band of harpies. Anastasia turned to double check how close she was to the edge, but she moved her head too fast. Her inner ear, still disrupted by the previous fall, betrayed her. The world spun anew.

She fell.

More tumbling. More darkness. More cries of the nameless one descending after her. When Anastasia finally landed, the only reason she was not dead—she was sure—was because she was in the spirit realm already. Maybe she was dead, now, and when—if—she returned to the Path, she would be caught in its upward flow, into the afterlife to be with her ancestors, Jesus, or whatever.

The bottom of the ravine was dusty and dark. Anastasia coughed and two blue lights appeared, casting the canyon in a dim glow. The nameless one closed in on her. In addition to the voices without meaning that poured from his gaping maw, she could now hear the flicker of the flames behind his eyes and the rubbing of his blue tongue on the insides of his teeth.

Anastasia *wished* she did have some superpower, like Esmeralda had said, but at the moment she knew she was helplessly ordinary. The Devourer's breath was foul, like flesh rotting from gangrene or fungus growing over a grave. It was as hot as sewer gas as well, yet her flesh was still covered in goosebumps, as if a wind blew on her from off a glacier.

Then something Latia had said came to her, and in the strange logic of a dream state, Anastasia put her hand up and said, "Wait . . . wait . . . let me tell you a story."

It was absurd, she knew it. But Latia had talked about the power of story. Dialogue was stronger than chaos, or so Anastasia hoped.

Whatever the case, the nameless one stopped, his giant mask hovering a mere arm's length from Anastasia's face. The wind of his breath, in and out, brushed against her cheeks and moved the ends of her hair.

He was waiting.

# ~ Part 1 ~

# Jamhuri the Proud & the Tree of the Sky

Jamhuri was afraid of nothing, and he was not afraid to say so. "I am Jamhuri Jumari, greatest warrior of the savannah," he would say. "I have defeated a lion in combat. I have outrun the cheetah in a race. I can throw my spear farther and I can leap higher than anybody."

The other young warriors of Jamhuri's community all grew tired of his bragging. When they saw him approaching, they would groan, "Jamhuri the Proud is coming to tell us how great he is—again!"

"Jamhuri the Proud?" one said to his friends. "More like Jamhuri the Loud!" Then they all broke into laughter behind Jamhuri's back.

Despite all his spectacular qualities, Jamhuri was surprised that the young women of his village smiled and laughed with the other young men, but not with him. When he came near, the young women became sullen and quiet. Then they would excuse themselves, suddenly remembering that they needed to tend to their chores, take care of their siblings, or catch up on important reading before the start of the next school term.

"School," Jamhuri scoffed. "Who needs *that!* None of these women are good enough for Jamhuri the Magnificent anyway," Jamhuri told himself. "Magnificent" was one of his favorite words to use when describing himself. He liked it almost as much as "glorious," "marvelous," and "superb." Jamhuri decided that only the most outstanding woman would be fit to be his companion.

And he knew exactly who she was: Latia Solei. Latia was the daughter of the village chief, Saitoti Solei. Latia was beautiful. It was said that she was so beautiful that Chief Saitoti, worried that admiring and lovesick boys would distract her from her studies, had hidden her away. He had found the highest acacia tree in all of the savannah, the *Mti wa Anga*—the Tree of the Sky—built a hut on top, with a giant antenna for WiFi, and sent Latia away to live there. The only people allowed in the tree were Latia's brothers and cousins to keep her company, as well as her tutors, her Judo instructor, and the Zen Master hired to teach Latia the arts of compassion, listening, and meditation.

So it was with an inward groan that Chief Saitoti finally allowed Jamhuri into a meeting of community elders to express his desire to make Latia his wife. Saitoti was a handsome and regal looking man, who sat tall on his tripod stool in his colorful carmine and indigo robes. His expression was often one of patience, and whoever sat before him in audience, felt that he listened as if they were the only two people in the world. His eyes were deep wells of compassion and wisdom; however, upon seeing Jamhuri approach, swaggering forward in long, haughty steps, dressed in outrageous apricot-colored robes, carrying his staff carved from baobab and topped with peacock feathers, the chief shrank down in his seat, his shoulders pinched inward. He had to work hard to restrain himself from closing his eyes, shaking his head, and putting his palm to his forehead.

"I am Jamhuri Jumari," the young man boasted, stomping his foot and striking the ground with his staff so that the feathers trembled. "I am as sly as a fox and as handsome as the rising sun. I will seek your daughter, and she will marry me."

Some of the elders coughed. Others cleared their throats and looked away or suddenly discovered an urgent reason to check their mobile phones. Chief Saitoti shifted in his seat, trying to find the right words to meet Jamhuri's without damaging what he knew to be a fragile ego.

While the chief uncharacteristically hesitated, one of the female elders, Mother Tabitha—a wise woman with turquoise wraps and amber jewelry—scoffed, unable to keep her disdain a secret any longer.

"Jamhuri, these are not the old days when a woman was the property of the men in her life. Why do you assume Latia would even have you as her companion, much less her husband?"

By all reports Latia was indeed a talented and educated young woman. Her father was regarded as a sagacious leader, so it was no surprise that she appeared to be on a similar path to wisdom. Jamhuri had realized it would take just such a woman to recognize his worth and be his equal, unlike the other foolish girls of his village and the neighboring ones that had rejected him. They were simply too intimidated by his greatness. He just needed to explain this to Mother Tabitha, whom he perceived to be a bit slow.

"Well, any woman as wise and outstanding as Latia, the daughter of Chief Saitoti, would surely recognize the king among men that I am," Jamhuri replied, without irony.

Now even Mother Tabitha could not find words. More precisely, she had plenty of words for Jamhuri and other young men just like him, she just didn't know where to start. Chief Saitoti, knowing there was more important business to attend to than Jamhuri and his foolishness, finally spoke up:

"I have heard of you, Jamhuri Jumari, Jamhuri the Proud. I have long expected you."

Jamhuri, if possible, stood up even straighter, his chest swelling even further. He took this to be a good sign. The chief continued.

"But Latia's affections are not mine to give, nor is it my right to choose which young man she is to spend time with . . . much less choose her husband. She is still young. She has many things she wants to do first. Her life is hers to live, her choices her own to make."

Jamhuri actually interpreted the chief's words as a hopeful sign and not a form of rejection, as Jamhuri was certain Latia would choose him. Why wouldn't she? After all, he was as splendid as the sunrise, as strong as an earthquake, and as charming as a minstrel.

"I will not stand in your way," Chief Saitoti continued. "But neither will I force any decision on my daughter. I placed her in the Mti wa Anga for a reason, the journey to reach her being a test in itself. So, first you will have to reach her, Jamhuri."

Chief Saitoti said this, thinking it would be the end of things with Jamhuri, for he knew no regular young man would be able to discover the way up into the highest reaches of the tree.

"A worthy test for a worthy man!" Jamhuri announced with a flourish, raising his staff to shake it and the peacock feathers with it.

The chief mumbled something no one else quite heard before he spoke up to dismiss the young man. "Uh, yes. Well, best of luck."

Jamhuri trekked many miles to the valley where the Mti wa Anga stood. Even he was surprised when he beheld its height. "Surely a tree so tall must touch the very sky," he said. "But it does not matter. I shall climb it, introduce myself, and upon meeting me, Latia will not be able to resist my charms."

But the way Latia's siblings, cousins, and tutors would reach her was a closely guarded secret. Jamhuri was not discouraged, even if he did not know it. He simply began to climb straight away, pulling himself up, swinging and leaping from branch to branch. As he climbed higher, he became tired. He struggled to stay upright and to balance upon the branches without falling. Monkeys watched him and spoke among themselves.

"Is that another young man trying to reach our lady Latia?"

"Shall we tell him the way up?"

"Let us ask him if he wants our help."

So the monkeys swung down to meet Jamhuri on his way up. By now he was weary from the arduous climb—although he would not admit it to himself—and seeing the ease with which the monkey's moved from branch to branch, he grew jealous; in his jealousy he grew irritable, the irritability growing to rage. When the monkeys finally came alongside him and offered their advice, Jamhuri spat back:

"I am Jamhuri the Outstanding! I don't need any help from dumb, silly monkeys."

"Suit yourself," the monkeys said, and they decided to leave Jamhuri to his own devices, returning up the tree with ease and grace he did not possess. This made Jamhuri even more angry. He continued to climb, to try to catch up with the monkeys, to prove that he was a better climber than they. He looked forward to reaching the crown of the tree and laughing at them. But as he continued to ascend, the air grew thin. He grew dizzy. Without a tail like a monkey, balancing on the smaller branches was difficult for Jamhuri. He took his steps more slowly, one by one, wrapping his arms around the trunk of the tree. Sweat dripped into his eyes. His mouth grew dry, and his limbs started to shake.

"Are you sure you don't want our help?" the monkeys called down.

"I don't need yours or anyone's stupid help," Jamhuri said, lifting his hand off a branch to make a fist and shake it at the monkeys.

That was when he fell.

Jamhuri tumbled down from one branch to another, striking them with a loud yowl each time, until he finally thumped on the hard, bare ground at the foot of the tree.

When Jamhuri came to, he was not about to let the monkeys have the last laugh. "I might not be able to climb like the monkeys," he said, "but I am still as sly as a fox and can leap like a gazelle."

Jamhuri spent the next few days gathering rushes and reeds, grasses and weeds. He began weaving a large, flexible mat. Some of his peers from his village came to watch and asked him what he was doing.

"What does it look like, you idiots? I will make a trampoline, and I will bounce high enough to reach the top of the tree."

A few asked among themselves why Jamhuri insisted on building a trampoline when he could order one online to be drone delivered the next day. But they decided Jamhuri probably did not want the suggestion. Instead they started filming him with their phones. One young man, Eustice, whose favorite subject was physics, offered to help Jamhuri calculate the distance he would need to run, his speed, and the force with which he would need to strike the trampoline mat. But Jamhuri shouted at him.

"You try to bamboozle me with numbers! Jamhuri is synonymous with genius. I don't need your physics, your force equations, or your trajectories." He said this last word in the same way he might say "halitosis" or "leprosy." So on Jamhuri went weaving, cutting the poles to hold the mat, and planting them in the ground.

"Suit yourself," Eustice said.

When Jamhuri was finished, he climbed up the nearest and highest hill. It was called Look Far Hill, and from its peak one could see the lands for miles and miles around. The only thing higher than it was the Mti wa Anga itself. Jamhuri started running down. His neighbors filmed while Eustice sat, his arms crossed and his head shaking, having already calculated the necessary parameters Jamhuri would need to land safely. Jamhuri built up speed until his apricot robes were flapping in the breeze. When he approached the trampoline, he jumped, his legs out in front of him, and aimed for its center.

He did indeed bounce high into the air, much to the astonishment of the spectators. The young men and women "Oooohhed" and "Aaaahhed," their necks craning back, their eyes squinting into the sun as Jamhuri shrank into a tiny dot in the sky that the cameras on their phones could not even detect. Eustice, unlike the others, looked down. He scratched a few more calculations in the dirt, double-checking his work. He arrived at the same solution as before and shook his head with a sigh.

Jamhuri flew towards the top of the tree, gaining such elevation that the air grew even colder and thinner than before. He passed the monkeys and made a face at them, for he was certain he had shown them that his brain was far superior to theirs. Jamhuri even came so close to the top of the tree that he could see the roof of the hut and even its antenna for WiFi. But before he could set foot on the top, he felt his momentum dispersing. He came to a gradual stop, balanced weightless in the air for the shortest of moments, then started to fall, still well short of the top of the tree. He fell, gaining speed, gaining momentum, and helpless to slow himself. The branches of the tree passed in a blur. He zoomed by the monkeys with a "WHOOSH," an apricot-colored blur. But they did not bother to look away from their grooming. The only thing that saved Jamhuri's life was a strong breeze that caught his billowing robes and pushed him into a river, where an angry hippo broke his fall. The hippo chased Jamhuri to the riverbank, where he scrambled away to safety and collapsed. Wet, bruised, and panting, he looked up to see Eustice, who was still shaking his head,

"Yep, this is just about where I calculated you would land."

"Leave me alone, Eustice," Jamhuri said. "You don't need to tell me 'I told you so.'"

"I didn't."

"Well, leave me alone anyway, you know-it-all."

"Suit yourself."

Jamhuri was still determined. As he walked home, he passed by a lake where he saw a flock of flamingos. They stalked through the shallows of blue water in broods of puffy pink feathers balanced on red, stick-like legs. That was when Jamhuri was struck with an idea. He went home to collect a thousand strings that he tied into tiny snares. Then he returned to the lake and chased after the flamingos, splashing after them in the water, screaming like a madman. When the graceful birds would take to the air to flee from him and his wild antics, Jamhuri lassoed their legs and held on to the string with a tight fist. After he had snared a great many, he cried, "Fly! Fly me to the top of the tree, you silly birds!"

But flamingos are vain creatures and do not like to do favors for people unless asked politely, which Jamhuri had not done. The flamingos, indeed, lifted Jamhuri into the air. They flew him higher and closer to the hut than he had been before. In fact, this time he was so close that he could see that the top of the tree was covered in a dusting of snow and that a series of windmills stood next to the hut, spinning in the wind to make power. He imagined he could even see a figure through the windows. She was reading at a desk and she turned her head at the sound of the commotion in the sky.

But the flamingos brought Jamhuri no closer. They soared over and past the hut, sweeping Jamhuri dangerously close to the windmill blades. He dodged and swung and tried to reach down to catch hold of the WiFi antenna as it passed, but the flamingos soared higher, scooping the air with their long wings. Jamhuri, although he would not have admitted this to anyone, grew scared as the flamingos flew so high he could see the edge of the earth curving away and the blue of the sky faded to a cold black, pinpricked by winking stars.

Then the flamingos tucked their wings and shot downward, like a cloud of flying darts. Jamhuri could barely breathe, the air rushed past him so fast. The curve of the horizon flattened, the air grew hot once more, and the earth rushed upwards. They passed through clouds of insects that struck Jamhuri's face with painful "splats," sending an oily, warm goo into his mouth and eyes. He started to cough and gag even as the ground grew closer. Just before they crashed, the flock of flamingos changed their direction, shooting up once more. The turn was too abrupt for Jamhuri's weight; his thin strings broke and he tumbled down, splashing into a bubbling sulfur lake.

Jamhuri could swear he heard the birds laughing as they flew off. In their voices he could hear the laughter of his village neighbors, the monkeys, and the elders. He wiped at the goo spread on his face, shook his fist, and went to cry out, "Stupid birds," only to choke on the bitter fumes from the sulfur lake that smelled of rotten eggs.

But Jamhuri was still determined, and from his passage through the heavens he had a new idea.

That evening, Jamhuri carried a rope and went to the moon, just as it was rising over a pasture where cows and buffalo grazed. Jamhuri called up to the heavenly body while it was still low and orange on the horizon, "Moon, Moon! Let me tie this rope around you. As you rise into the sky, you will carry me to the top of the highest tree. Then I can reach Latia and make her my wife."

The moon heard, but the moon is not a friendly orb. Most nights he is angry, because everyone comes out during the day to work and play under the sun; but when he rises, only a few people appreciate his beauty while most go to bed—even though, without him, there would be no tides, no tidal pools, and the currents and waves of the oceans would be dull and boring.

The moon replied, speaking in an imperious tone that would have been familiar to Jamhuri, had he possessed any self-awareness whatsoever (which he didn't): "What have you done for me, haughty human? You have never watched me cross the night sky in all my majesty. You sleep like the others. No, sleepy human, I will not help you."

Jamhuri remained determined. He returned to his mat at the base of Look Far Hill. The spectators had retired to their homes and their schools some time before. Their videos of Jamhuri hurtling through the sky and landing in a river had garnered thousands of comments, likes, and "wows" on various social media platforms. But everyone had departed except for Eustice, who, seeing Jamhuri return to the hill, came out to offer him help.

"How many times do I need to tell you, I don't need your help!" Jamhuri said. "I'm going to repurpose these reeds and grasses into a sling, set it between two trees, and fling myself to the top of the tree."

Eustice sighed, "Suit yourself, Jamhuri."

Jamhuri did as he said he would do, setting the sling between two baobab trees. He sat himself in the pouch in the center and walked the sling backwards, stretching it as he went. It stretched and stretched until the trees themselves were straining, until Jamhuri's feet were blistered from holding the sling back, and *still* he pulled. The monkeys, the flamingos, the hippo, and the moon watched. Even Eustice looked up from a set of new equations as he scratched them in a note pad and calculated on his phone. Still, Jamhuri pulled the sling even farther. Eustice adjusted his calculations to compensate, looking down at the grass bending in the wind to estimate the wind speed. Jamhuri aimed himself between two stars. Eustice shook his head and sighed. Jamhuri let go.

The sling flung him with a giant snap. He flew through more clouds of bugs and even the bats that were out to eat them that evening. He soared over the river and the angry hippo, the lake and the vain flamingos. He made a rude hand gesture at the monkeys bedding down for the night as he passed. He was elated as he soared towards the top of the tree. He soared like a rocket. He felt the cold air on his skin and saw the sparkle of the snow in the moonlight. This time he was certain he saw a figure watching him from the door of the hut, her head tilted in curiosity.

But Jamhuri had aimed too high. He passed over the tree and flew towards the moon. And the moon, in his own curiosity, had moved too close.

They collided, the foolish young man and the conceited moon. It was such a collision that Jamhuri was knocked senseless. It is said that the moon wavered in his orbit and, to this day, still bears a crater from where Jamhuri slammed into him. Jamhuri fell to the earth and only survived because Eustice had calculated the place where Jamhuri would land. In that place, Eustice had taken what was left of the trampoline and woven the pieces into a net, which caught Jamhuri and saved his life.

When Jamhuri woke up, he saw Eustice standing next to the net.

"You don't need to thank me," Eustice said.

"I won't! I would have done it if the moon had not gotten in my way."

"Of course you would have," Eustice said, shaking his head.

Many people thought Jamhuri would quit after such a close brush with death. They thought he would be humbled. But Jamhuri was not humbled. He was not chastened. He was as determined and arrogant as ever. He was also bruised and cut and he ached all over.

He had lost his sandals, his robes were torn, and his staff with the peacock feathers was missing.

"Perhaps for this task I need to turn to the gods. After all, they are the wisest of all beings, and they are likely to see what a worthy man I am."

So Jamhuri fell upon his knees and prayed to his ancestors. He prayed for wind, a wind like that which blew across the grasslands before the rains, a wind so powerful that it would bear him to the top of the tree.

Then Jamhuri danced. He danced for days and he danced for nights. He danced without food. He danced without water. He danced without rest.

"How long will this go on?" the monkeys asked the hippo, who then asked the flamingos, who then asked the moon.

"I do not know," replied the moon, who pretended not to care but had moved very close to see what would happen, despite his surface still being sore and cratered from his collision with Jamhuri.

The neighbors gathered around Jamhuri's home and whispered among themselves, wondering what would happen next. They all could hear Jamhuri praying to the gods in a fervent voice. Eustice looked on and shook his head, saying, "Jamhuri should be careful; sometimes the gods' justice is to give us just what we ask for. . ."

"Whatever do you mean?" someone asked Eustice.

But Eustice just shook his head and said, "We'll see."

After many days, the sky darkened. The clouds gathered, the grasses bent, and the trees shrugged in the wind. Jamhuri's prayer had been answered. A windstorm like none other came rolling across the grasslands. It had the power of a herd of elephants and the speed of a cheetah. It lifted the thatch eaves of the houses and sent the people and animals of the savannah into hiding. Elands, ibises, klipspringers, hartebeests, wildebeests, waterbucks, warthogs, warblers, hornbills, shoebills, rhinos, servals, zebras, gazelles, dik-diks, pipits, egrets, kudus, and kestrels—all cowered, all hid. Except for Jamhuri. Jamhuri did not hide. He did not cower. Jamhuri raced out to meet the wind.

It struck him like an ocean wave and tumbled him upward. After days and nights of dancing, forgoing food and water, Jamhuri's body was light and flew like a leaf. "I'm a leaf on the wind!" he laughed as he rose, for he knew he had found favor with the gods. The monkeys, the hippo, the flamingos, the moon, and the villagers watched with wide eyes as Jamhuri climbed higher and higher, lifted as if by invisible hands, past the highest boughs, up into the colder air, to finally land on top of the tree.

The dusting of snow was cold beneath Jamhuri's toes, and his skin soon became covered with goosebumps. In his threadbare robes, which had become so battered and torn from his adventures, Jamhuri shivered. The door to the hut opened, and out stepped the most beautiful young woman he had ever seen. She was followed by her retinue of teachers and tutors. A stocky woman with long limbs—the Judo instructor—followed as well. Behind her was an old man—the Zen master—his gray beard braided with purple bows.

But Jamhuri barely noticed them. He had eyes only for Latia. Her skin was like ebony that glowed with a golden sheen. Her eyes shone with the sparkle of moonlight in raindrops. Her hair was adorned with beads of a thousand colors. The bangles on her wrists and ankles chimed like music. She walked with grace and power.

At first Jamhuri could not find words. His heart beat so hard, he feared his ribs would come loose. But as the silence lengthened and Latia and her mentors looked on, he managed to stutter and say, "I-I-I am Jamhuri the Mighty!" Jamhuri's voice cracked in a very unmanly manner as he spoke. He stretched his neck out as he swallowed the nervous lump in his throat. He decided to remind everyone present of his accomplishments up to that point: "I have tamed the flamingos, humbled the moon, and ridiculed my doubters and detractors. Now, Latia, I am here to make you *mine*."

At first, his words were met with stone silence, the grownups looking from one to another out of the corners of their eyes. Some mumbled and whispered to each other, but they all seemed to wait upon what Latia would say.

And when she spoke, she laughed—a note of derision in her voice that struck Jamhuri in his chest like an arrow. "Tamed the flamingos? Humbled the moon? Ridiculed your detractors?" Latia's eyes, those shining, luminous eyes, grew wide and incredulous before they narrowed. "I saw something much different. I saw a fool put in his place by a flock of birds. I saw a reckless young man crash into the moon. And I saw an arrogant boy insult his neighbors and alienate every last person and animal who offered him help. You are not Jamhuri the Brilliant, but Jamhuri the Brash."

Jamhuri stood, feeling as if he was growing smaller, sinking into the top of tree. His body felt emptied out, his skin thin, exposed. But Latia had not finished. "And you are not outstandingly magnificent but rather outrageously mistaken if you think any woman, any person 'belongs' to another."

Jamhuri blinked his eyes, for his vision had grown blurry. He checked his feet, for now he felt like he was falling once again, but he saw that the sturdy platform of branches still held him in place. Perhaps it was just the wind in his eyes and the long days without food or drink making him dizzy. . .

Latia concluded her words to him, "But I will say this, Jamhuri the Foolhardy: my father always said to me that the day a young man reached the top of the tree would be the day I was ready to leave, to go off to see the world. So for that I guess I must thank you."

Jamhuri was not sure as to what was happening next, for Latia turned to her mentors, hugging them each, one by one. There were a few tears, as there might be at a good-bye or a graduation. One of the teachers brought Latia a traveling bag, stuffed full of books, clothes, and writing pads. A second teacher came walking beneath a pink cloud. Its edges moved, and its center swam before Jamhuri's eyes. It took him a moment to realize the cloud was actually the same flock of flamingos that he had tried to lasso. But this time they were indeed tamed and waited obediently as Latia took the ribbon of strings and asked the flamingos, with impeccable courtesy, to bear her away. They answered with joyful squawks, then they tilted their wings, drawing Latia up and out of Jamhuri's reach. As she passed before the stars, Latia cried out, "You are a handsome boy, Jamhuri! But only a boy. You need to grow up—if you can. I'm curious what kind of man you will be. Maybe when I return, we might find out. Or maybe not. You can wait and see if you like . . . or not."

Latia's laugh faded into the night.

The monkeys felt pity for Jamhuri and helped him down from the tree, as did the moon who remained up in the night sky longer than usual to light the way. The normally grumpy hippo felt heartbroken for Jamhuri and carried him to the village. When the sun came up, Jamhuri went directly to Chief Saitoti and his circle of elders. Jamhuri told his story. The chief and elders listened. When Jamhuri finished, Chief Saitoti spoke, "I raised my daughter to be an independent woman. Perhaps I should have given you more warning."

"I . . . I don't know if I would have listened," Jamhuri said.

The elders said nothing, stunned into silence by this rare admission on Jamhuri's part. Chief Saitoti stroked his chin, studying

Jamhuri, as if trying to determine if something in the young man had indeed changed. "How will you spend your energies now, young warrior?"

Jamhuri reflected for a moment, remembering Latia's words, her accusation that he'd been "brash," "arrogant," and having "alienated" his neighbors. It was no use pursuing other young women. Jamhuri knew now none would want to spend time in his company. Jamhuri had no male friends; he had never bothered to make friends with them, since he had felt them so beneath him. And there were few elders who would mentor him, because he had so often spurned their advice.

"I'm not sure, my chief. Perhaps it is time I spent some time with myself."

And so Jamhuri did. Many moons passed. Jamhuri built himself a home. He began with a fence of sharpened sticks and thorns to protect his goats, chickens, and cows. The fence was higher than any other in the village in order keep out predators such as leopards and lions.

"Why does Jamhuri build such a high fence?" the young men asked each other.

"Probably so he can boast that he has the highest fence in the village," they scoffed.

But Jamhuri told them, "I built it high to keep out the crafty cats of the savannah."

"No cat can leap that high," the other young men said.

"I did once," Jamhuri said softly. "So a lion might learn, too."

Next, he built a house within the fence. It was a great house with room for a large family, even though Jamhuri did not have a family, and most of the rooms remained empty.

The neighbors came by and laughed. "Look at Jamhuri the Proud. He cannot even find a friend to live in his giant house with him!"

Jamhuri had no reply. He wondered if he would indeed live in that big house alone forever. He worked during the days and spent his lonely evenings reading books and teaching himself the school lessons he had scoffed at others for learning years before.

A few moons later, a pack of wily lions raided the village and killed many cows. Every family suffered terrible losses, except Jamhuri, whose herd was left intact thanks to his high fence. To help his neighbors, even the ones who had mocked him, Jamhuri gave calves away as gifts.

"Jamhuri the Prudent," he heard a few people say.

"Jamhuri the Generous."

"Jamhuri the Gracious," others said.

A few more moons passed. For a time the rains were good, and the people repaid Jamhuri with gifts of pottery, spears, and marvelous headdresses. Some gave him scratch cards for airtime on his mobile phone, but the minutes only accumulated, as he had no friends to call. Seeing that he was becoming very rich, a few fathers urged their daughters to marry Jamhuri, but Jamhuri turned them all down.

"Latia was right; I am too boastful and arrogant to be a husband to anyone," he said.

So the people left Jamhuri alone. But they gave him yet another name. They called him Jamhuri the Pitiful.

Jamhuri took good care of his herd. Because others often poked fun at him, he did not mind taking his herd on long trips into the savannah that would keep him away from the village for many days at a time. In this way Jamhuri learned of the most fertile pastures and the most refreshing watering holes. He taught himself to read the land, the sky, and the movement of animals to predict the weather, navigate the wilderness, and avoid danger. His cows and sheep grew healthy, and Jamhuri learned the land better than anyone else in his community.

Then came the day when Eustice, who had married and become a father, could not find his children. They were twins, a boy and a girl, and they had not returned home from school one afternoon. The village sent out search parties, but no one could find them, and it was feared that a leopard had stalked and eaten them. The people gave up searching, but Eustice held out hope. He came to Jamhuri's house and fell on his knees, weeping.

"Jamhuri, I know you have roamed the lands wider than anyone in our village. You know the grasslands and acacia forests even from the skies above. Can you help me find my children?"

Jamhuri helped Eustice up, remembering how Eustice had helped him and saved his life when he had been so brash and arrogant before. "Of course I will help you, Eustice. You offered me friendship when no one else would. I repaid it with rudeness and without thanks."

Jamhuri set out immediately, wandering many days and many nights, farther than anyone else had been willing to go to search for the twins. He was rewarded, for he found signs of their trail and tracked their prints over many days. He kept up hope, and in time he found the twins. They had been chased by a pack of hyenas and climbed a tree for safety. Jamhuri chased the pack of hyenas away, rescued the twins from the tree, and returned them to their home, safe and sound.

"Jamhuri the Persistent," the villagers cried joyously when Jamhuri returned with the sister and brother. Eustice and his wife thanked him many times over.

When Jamhuri realized that the walk to school was too long and too dangerous, he decided to convert the extra rooms in his home to classrooms. Jamhuri moved to a smaller, modest hut in the back. His compound became a school for the village community, and with the help of Eustice, he ran a cable to the WiFi on the top of the Mti wa Anga where Latia had lived, so that the students would have access to all the best learning from all over the globe. The students thrived and won science and essay contests from all around the world. They went off to university where they wrote poems and plays, made friends and discoveries, and crafted new inventions to improve the world. Together, Jamhuri and Eustice also created a library to gather the wisdom and knowledge of the elders, whom they sought out to hear their stories and record their memories for posterity, preserving their legacies for future generations. Eustice helped to digitize the information so it could be shared with the wider world through their Mti wa Anga uplink.

Many busy days passed, turning into weeks, months, and even years. One day, Chief Saitoti came to visit Jamhuri after he had finished teaching classes. A long time had passed since they had last met. Jamhuri had been busy running the school. The chief had even stepped down and handed his duties over to Mother Tabitha, who ran the village with prudence and wisdom. Jamhuri offered Chief Saitoti some rooibos tea, and they sat around the fire.

"Jamhuri, your house is sturdy, your school is a success, and you are well loved in the community. Fortune has smiled upon you. It shall be a clear night tonight, and the stars will be bright. Maybe tonight you should walk to Look Far Hill and see what you can see."

"I will go because you ask me to, my chief. But I must admit, many nights I look into the sky and remember the night Latia left. I remember the words she spoke to me, naming me, rightly, as brash and arrogant, and reminding me how selfish I had been."

The chief turned his teacup in his hand and, after a moment, answered. "It was a sad night for you, I remember that, young man. But sometimes the worst parts of our stories are actually the beginnings of something better."

Jamhuri was not sure what the chief meant, but he promised to keep his word. He walked to Look Far Hill later that night. As Jamhuri walked, his heart was heavy. He had looked into the sky more times that he cared to count in the past years, each time remembering how foolish he had been in years past and how his pride had driven Latia away. As he walked now, he noticed the monkeys in the trees. "Strange," he said to himself. "They seem to be watching me."

When he passed the old grumpy hippo in the river, he noticed it was not sleeping. Instead, it snorted and hissed, wiggling its ears and playing along with its companions. Even the moon was out, so bright and so full that Jamhuri could see the snow sparkling upon the crown of the Mti wa Anga. As he gazed up at the darkened hut—its teachers and their student long gone—he heard a fluttering on the breeze. He turned his face up to the starry sky and realized the sound was that of flamingo wings beating against the wind. A great flock of the birds eclipsed the stars and the moon, their feathers pink and silver under its light. On a silk swing that dangled below the graceful flamingos rode Latia.

The birds circled the hill before swooping down to let Latia off. She set a bejeweled foot decorated with henna upon the ground. She was as beautiful as Jamhuri remembered, but now she wore a crown of platinum in her plaited hair. Her eyes were lined with kohl; her hands and feet were bestrewn with ribbons that fluttered in the breeze.

"Let it be sung from the mountaintop," she said, "that Princess Latia has returned. I have visited the Pharaoh's tomb in Cairo. I have read in the great library of Alexandria. I have walked among the pillars of Carthage. I have bartered in the great market of Timbuktu. I have wandered the stone towns of Lamu and the spice gardens of Zanzibar. I have danced with the holy priestesses of Dahomey, wept at the Door of No Return, and paid homage at the Door of Return. I have ascended into the secret churches of the Coptics, and I have descended into the glittering mines of the Matswana. I have set eyes upon the Gold Coast, the Ivory Coast, and even the Skeleton Coast, and lived to tell of it. I have seen where the great oceans end, where they begin, and where they meet. Now I have returned to tell my story."

When she had finished, her voice echoed into the empty night. Somewhere a cricket chirped. Latia looked around. "Is there no one here to meet me?" she asked in a softer voice. A tear appeared in the corner of her eye and smeared the kohl painted there.

"I am here," a single voice answered.

"What? Where are the others?"

"Tending their herds, cooking their meals, and teaching their children," Jamhuri replied. "A village life is a full one."

"Who are you?" Latia asked.

"Some call me Jamhuri the Patient; others call me Jamhuri the Prudent. Some call me Jamhuri the Persistent, others Jamhuri the Pitiful. You once knew me as Jamhuri the Proud."

When Latia recognized the man standing before her, she was confused.

"But Jamhuri, you were once so . . . arrogant and loud."

"You are right, and it brought me nothing but isolation. Now I have tried to live my life for others and not myself. Our neighbors in the village are resting and sleeping from a long day. We should respect their time for quiet and not disturb them. We will wake them in the morning, but now, come sit with me by the fire and tell me of your stories. I will listen."

And so she did. Latia spent the whole night recounting her adventures to Jamhuri over rooibos tea. He remained awake for all of it, listening with an eager heart and attentive ears. Latia was stunned at the transformation she perceived in Jamhuri; this once boastful young man had become a selfless listener and dutiful friend to his neighbors. Latia, who had grown a bit prideful herself, realized that perhaps there was something she could learn from him. In the morning they went out, and the villagers leapt from their beds at the news Latia had returned. The following night there was a great feast to celebrate her homecoming. After the meal and the dancing, all gathered around as Latia told of her travels to the most distant reaches of Africa. But Latia also made time to listen to the villagers as they shared news of their lives and the achievements of their children.

As Latia sat beside him, Jamhuri felt proud. But it was a different kind of proud, because it was for another person and not himself. He liked this feeling much better. So he remained next to

Latia, content and quiet. Many friends, neighbors, and elders—especially Chief Saitoti—noticed how, between the stories, Latia would look with smiling eyes on Jamhuri. For once, Jamhuri did not care if anyone paid him any attention. Surrounded by neighbors he could call friends and elders he could call mentors, he did not need any attention at all. He was happy simply to listen.

And that is how Jamhuri the Proud became Jamhuri the Wise.

# ~ Part 2 ~

# Njambi, the Littlest Daughter

In the village of Kaliande, a peaceful community settled between the floating escarpments of the Great Rift Valley and in the shadow of Mount Kaliande, the old man Murito was sick. He had tried many herbal remedies and modern medicines. He had bathed in a bath of lavender. He had breathed in the smoke of burning eucalyptus. He had worn sacred beads around his neck. He had poured libations on the ground in offering to his ancestors. He had drunk palm wine mixed with rooibos tea. He had rubbed palm oil on his aching joints. When none of those things worked, he drank cow's milk. And when that did not work, he drank cow's blood. He had also tried ibuprofen, paracetamol, penicillin, amoxicillin, erythromycin, tetracycline, ciprofloxacin, fluoxetine, fluvoxamine, paroxetine, citalopram, and many other medicines that had names that seemed like the whole alphabet jumbled into new permutations and combinations that made no sense.

Still, Murito did not improve. When Dr. Chege, Murito's old friend who was a doctor and a shaman, came to visit, he examined Murito. When Dr. Chege finished, he sat in silence, stroking his beard. During that time, Murito's wife, Niobi, and his four daughters—Gathoni, the eldest; Wanjiku, the second; Shiro, the third; and Njambi, the littlest daughter—waited with anxious eyes, knitted brows, and folded hands.

Finally, Dr. Chege spoke. "Murito, you are very ill. Your cure is beyond my skills as a physician and even as a shaman. But as a shaman, I believe I know what would heal you: a drink from the Water of Life."

"The Water of Life?" Murito exclaimed. "But that is only a myth."

Dr. Chege nodded, his expression solemn. "Sometimes, old friend, there is more truth in myth than in fact. That is the prescription I will leave you with this morning: imagination is more crucial than knowledge, curiosity more important than certainty, and wonder is the beginning of wisdom."

Murito nodded, but looked as troubled and perplexed as Njambi, the littlest daughter, felt listening. By the look on Njambi's mother and sisters' faces, she could tell they felt the same way. Shamans often spoke in riddles, and the riddles Dr. Chege shared that morning seemed less useful than a bottle of pills or a syringe of vaccine. But, as custom dictated, everyone remained polite and respectful, Murito most of all, thanking his old friend Dr. Chege and wishing him a safe journey home. But immediately upon the doctor's departure, Njambi's mother and sisters fell down at Murito's feet weeping, certain that they would soon be losing him.

Each of Njambi's sisters wailed louder than the next, each insisting that she would be most heartbroken over the loss of their father. It was not unusual for them to compete in this manner, and Njambi, being the youngest and smallest, often could not even make her voice heard in these debates, much less squeeze between her sisters as they formed a tight ring around their father, taking turns between their tears suggesting what items their father might leave them in his will.

Sad, Njambi shuffled outside where she noticed Dr. Chege's figure receding down the road. She decided to chase after him, running the length of the village, finally catching his attention by tugging on his sleeve.

"Dr. Chege, isn't there some medicine you can give my father, an oil or balm, or even a charm or spell that you can use?"

Dr. Chege smiled down at her, his eyes twinkling. "Oh Njambi, you are a good and loving daughter. I can see how worried you are, but everyone must face their frailty, even the inevitability of their mortality."

Njambi thought for a moment and realized that Dr. Chege must have to confront and tell people the bad news that they were ill or even dying every day. She wondered aloud, "Dr. Chege, what is it like for people to know that they are dying?"

Dr. Chege laughed, but his voice was gentle. "What is it like to pretend you are not?"

At this Njambi's heart felt a little colder. She did her best to put on a brave face, but a lump was forming in her throat. Dr. Chege, seeing her frown, spoke up. "But there is hope for your father, the Water of Life—"

"But it's just a story," Njambi said, biting her tongue, because she knew it was rude to interrupt adults.

"Ah, yes, but some stories have kernels of truth."

More riddles. Njambi found herself digging her nails into her palm, her frustration a flare rising inside her to rival her sadness. She bit her tongue again, afraid she might cry or afraid she might say something else rude to Dr. Chege. Again, as if he were reading her innermost thoughts, he patted her on the shoulder. "Dear Njambi, don't take life so seriously—it's not permanent."

Then he turned and made his way down the road.

When Njambi returned to her home, her mother was weeping silent tears while her sisters were still pushing and shoving to be the closest to her father's feet, each with a list of things they wanted to inherit.

"Oh my," Murito cried. "Will I ever be well again!"

"Perhaps one of our daughters might go to seek the Water of Life," Njambi's mother, Niobi, suggested.

"Yes, father, one of us can go seek it," Gathoni, the eldest daughter, said. She thought herself the best daughter and was always looking for ways to prove herself over her sisters and gain their father's favor.

"According to legend," Murito said, "The spring that feeds the pool where the Water of Life can be found, is high atop Kaliande Mountain."

"But Kaliande is so far, through the forest, across the river, and through the desert," Wanjiku, the second oldest, said.

"And the mountain is very high," Shiro, the third daughter, added.

"It will be a long and dangerous journey, yes," Murito said, his voice sad, for he did not want to ask his daughters to take on such a perilous quest for him.

"I will do it," Gathoni said, standing up and marching to the doorway. "And then you will know that I am your favorite and best daughter, and you can give to me our family cows so I can start a dairy business."

Although Njambi could see her sisters shoot resentful gazes Gathoni's way, no one said anything to object. It was not a time for arguing with their father so ill. Gathoni had always been the most responsible sister, so perhaps it was best that she go search for the Water of Life.

"Very well," Murito said. "Go with my blessing."

Gathoni turned, put on her sandals and head wrap, and started off for Mount Kaliande.

Gathoni set off down the road and, not long after, reached the acacia forest. Many people of their community were afraid of the forest, for it was said trickster spirits lived there, as well as dangerous animals. But as Gathoni came under the yellow lattice of acacia branches, with their emerald leaves and white thorns, she found the forest quite beautiful. She pulled out her phone and began to take pictures of herself with the flora and fauna in the background so that she could post and boast in her social media profiles. As she was taking a picture of herself, she nearly tripped over a young boy along the side of the road.

The boy was dressed in ragged clothes and had no shoes on. She knew there were poor people who were not "civilized" that lived around the forest. She imagined this boy was one of those backwards people. He was holding his foot, which was red and swollen.

"Help me, please," he said. "A bee has stung my heel. I need some balm to soothe it so I may walk again."

"I am very sorry," Gathoni said, "but I am already helping my father and I do not have time to help you. Maybe you should think of wearing some shoes, so you do not get stung next time."

Gathoni left the boy and continued into the forest, scrolling through her phone to pick the best filter for her latest photo. So engrossed was she in her decision on "Valencia filter" and bubbling with the excitement of how many likes she would get from her friends, she didn't notice how the forest became thicker, the trees denser, and their leaves blacker and more leathery, their thorns growing longer and dagger-like. It was only when the forest was so thick that it blotted out the daylight and Gathoni had to adjust the light on her screen that she realized she might have lost her way.

"Oh my, I think I might have wandered off the trail. . ."

Gathoni checked the GPS on her phone but saw, with a flutter of panic in her chest, that she no longer had reception. She began to look around and call out for help. No one answered, and yet, she felt as if she were being watched. She tried to retrace her steps along the forest paths, but she had not been paying attention to the twists, turns, and the landmarks that distinguished them. (Her phone had just seemed much more interesting at the time).

As Gathoni became more lost and more terrified, she thought she heard a rustling in the bushes. The leaves and branches suddenly exploded and a leopard leapt out at her, swinging its claws and grinning a terrible, hungry smile full of sharp teeth.

"Aiiiiieeeeeee!" Gathoni screamed. All sorts of birds were scared out of the trees and took to the sky. Wagtails stopped their wagging. Panicked hornbills made a noise like horns blowing. Tinker birds stopped their tinkering, and go-away birds . . . well . . . quickly went away.

Gathoni ran screeching and tearing through the underbrush. The thorns scratched her, tore her dress, and snagged her hair. Somehow, with enough running, she stumbled her way out of the woods. When she recognized where she was, she started back to the village. But when she neared her family's home, she realized that she had failed to find the Water of Life. Instead, she filled the bottle she had brought with her from the stream beside the village and brought it home.

Everyone was shocked to see Gathoni so disheveled, scratched, and bloody when she arrived home. She refused to talk about her journey and simply handed the bottle of water to their father. Murito thanked her, pulled out the cork, then drank the water. But he felt no better. "Maybe it was from the wrong spring," Murito said, disappointed.

"No matter," Gathoni said. "I tried." Then she left with her family's cows to start up her dairy business.

After Gathoni had departed, Niobi turned to Wanjiku. "Wanjiku, you are the smartest of all our daughters. Surely you can find the spring that holds the Water of Life, even if Gathoni could not."

"I will try," Wanjiku said, "but now that Gathoni has taken all our cows, how will I know that father loves me?"

"Your father and I love you very much, but if you need proof, perhaps we can give you my loom, which I use to make scarves, skirts, and robes."

"That would be perfect," Wanjiku said, jumping up, for she loved to weave and the loom was on the top of her list of items she wanted to inherit. She danced around the house retrieving her sandals, delighted at the thought of the money she would make, weaving her own fabrics and selling them online.

Wanjiku followed a route that led her to the Kaliande River first. She stood awestruck for a few moments, taking in its shimmering waters and serpentine banks that unfolded like a silk scarf cast across the shoulders of the world. As Wanjiku walked, looking for a place shallow enough to ford, she daydreamed of the beautiful skirts, scarves, and wraps she planned to make on the loom and the e-commerce empire she would run. Lost in her thoughts, she was startled to hear a woman call for help.

The woman was standing along the riverbank in water that reached just under her knees. She had a graceful figure, bent at the waist, and a strong back without any sway in it. Her arms were thrust into the water as if she were searching for something. Closer up, Wanjiku could see that the woman's face was creased with deep lines of worry. When she spoke, her voice was fraught with despair.

"I have dropped my water pot into the river," the woman said. "We do not have access to safe water in our home, so without this pot I cannot quench the thirst of my children, cook for them, or help them wash their hands. Kind young lady, can you please help me find it?"

"I'm sorry you dropped your water pot," Wanjiku said, "but I am already helping my father, and I must be hurrying on so I can get home and receive my very own loom. I'm starting an e-commerce business, you know. Maybe you will learn to be more careful next time."

Wanjiku, realizing that this would be a good place to cross, left the woman behind and began to wade across the river.

As Wanjiku walked, the water rose around her. It began at her ankles and moved up past her shins, her knees, and then to her waist. She had to take careful steps to keep moving across without being pushed downstream. The current grew stronger. It soon became difficult for Wanjiku to keep her footing. Now the water was up to her chest and just under her armpits. She was not a good swimmer, and she prayed the water would rise no higher. To her horror, as she took another step, she felt something long and slithery wrap itself around her legs.

"Eeeeeeeeeek!" she screamed. "A snake has gotten me!" She thrashed about in the water, punching and clawing at the snake, which she was *sure* was a river python and would pull her under to drown her then swallow her whole. She screamed for help, looking for the woman she had left at the riverbank to ask her for help, but she was nowhere to be seen. Each time Wanjiku tried to move to the safety of the opposite bank the python squeezed tighter, but when she moved backwards, to the bank she had started from, the python's coils became looser. Wanjiku cried and wiggled and kicked, moving in the direction of the shore. Finally, the terrible snake let her go, but after another step, she plunged into deeper water that swept her away. She bobbed and screamed again, splashing and treading water until she finally felt the riverbed under her feet. She scrambled for land, crawled up the bank, and collapsed flat on her face.

"Enough of this," she said, checking to make sure the python did not follow her and wringing out her clothes. "It's no use trying to cross this river." When she was a bit drier, she scooped some of the river water into the same bottle Gathoni had carried and went home to her parents.

"This water is certainly fresh. It tastes of sunlight, soft rain, and melted snow, but I feel no better," Murito said after drinking.

"I am very sorry, Father," Wanjiku said, already gathering up the pieces of the loom and packing them into her bags. "I suppose I chose the wrong stream as well." Then, with her bags slung over her shoulders, Wanjiku left to start her own business like her sister before her.

Murito and Niobi turned to Shiro. "Shiro, you are the most beautiful of my daughters, and I am sure you will go out to win many hearts," said Niobi. "But first, for your father's sake, will you go and search for the Water of Life?"

"Of course," Shiro said. "But only if you promise me all of our furniture and your mobile phone. I will need these things as I set up my own recording studio and become a famous singer."

"I promise you all those things, if you can help to save your father," Niobi said, even though Murito looked sad at the thought of having nothing left of his own.

"Very well," Shiro said.

Shiro took a circuitous route to Mount Kaliande, her path leading her first to the desert. On the edge of the desert, she met an old man. He was tall with a smooth, hairless head and lines in his face and scars on his hands that spoke of wisdom and experience.

"Help me, young one," he said. "I have just crossed the desert, and I am so thirsty."

"I have water in my calabash here," Shiro said. "But I need it, since I am crossing the desert myself."

And so she left the old man.

But once Shiro entered the desert, a great wind descended from the sky and struck her like a slap to her face. It did not relent. She had to lean just to keep walking upright. Her skirts whipped around her, and her head wrap flew away. Dust filled the air and made it impossible to see. Sand stung her skin like needles. It burned in her nose and scratched at her throat. It made her eyes water and left a bitter taste in her mouth as if she were being buried alive.

"This is unbearable!" Shiro cried and turned back.

When she reached her village, she poured the water from her calabash into the bottle meant for the Water of Life and offered it to her father.

Her father drank. "Thank you. This water tastes bitter, like strong medicine, but I feel no better," he said with a sigh.

"I suppose I picked the wrong spring too. What a shame," Shiro said, dragging the family table out the door, followed by each of the chairs. As she took the last one, she put her new phone to her ear and began to speak to her agent.

Murito leaned back into his bed, waiting to die. Niobi sat down beside him, took his hands, and wept.

Njambi, the littlest daughter, would normally be helping to prepare supper, but the table on which to eat was gone and so were the chairs for sitting. There were no cows to tend to and no loom for her to help her mother make fabrics. She went to her mother and father and said:

"Mother, Father, I will go and find the spring with the Water of Life."

"But Njambi, you are our littlest daughter. You are too small and too young for such a task," Niobi said.

"But there is no one else, and I must try for father's sake," Njambi said.

So Njambi left and started down the road towards the distant peak of Mount Kaliande, its craggy head surrounded by frosty clouds. Soon enough, the mountain peak was hidden from view as Njambi walked under the boughs of the acacia forest. She enjoyed the forest, for she liked to watch the flycatchers, the kestrels, and the sunbirds. Since there was not a mobile phone left among her and her parents, she walked along taking in the sights, letting them imprint on her mind instead of a memory card. She valued the views and sights all the more, for she realized she would never experience them quite the same way again.

As Njambi walked, she heard a voice.

"Please help me."

She turned and saw a boy sitting on the ground. He was in simple clothes that looked threadbare. Njambi was moved, for she imagined he must have been very poor. He was holding his foot and looked to be in anguish.

"What's wrong?" Njambi asked.

"I have been stung by a bee. My foot is too swollen for me to walk, and no one will help me." The boy began to weep. "I fear I might die here."

"Don't be afraid," Njambi said, kneeling down beside him. She examined his foot and saw that the bee's stinger was still lodged there. She drew it out with a gentle touch like her mother would use. "See, this is all that was the matter. You will feel better soon."

"Thank you," said the boy. "I can see the swelling is already going down. I hope you have a safe journey!"

Njambi continued through the forest. The branches overhead grew thick and the light weak. Soon it was as dark as night. Njambi tried to remain brave, but she felt scared in the dark as the sounds of strange animals and insects rose up in a nocturnal chorus. Her heart beat loudly in her chest. When she heard a rustling in the bushes, she was sure she would faint with fright.

The branches parted with a snapping noise. Njambi was prepared to run away when she realized that the noise had been made by a starling. It was one of the most beautiful starlings Njambi had ever seen. Its feathers gleamed like jewels, and its song was sweet like a flute. It fluttered slowly down the path and bounced there on its short little legs.

"I think it wants me to follow it," Njambi said. She decided it couldn't hurt. So she did. The starling led Njambi to the edge of the river. It was late now and too dark to cross, so Njambi wrapped herself in her *kikoi* and slept.

In the morning, Njambi opened her eyes to a clear sky. She could see Mount Kaliande in a brand-new pallet of colors: snow of rose, stone of blue, and a skirt of emerald forest. The orange ball of the sun perched on the mountain's shoulder. Njambi took in the view until her stomach began to grumble. She picked some mangos and ate them for breakfast as a flock of sacred ibis alighted at the river's edge and a lavender crane came stalking through the water looking for fish. While she sat on the riverbank, a tall woman came striding through the shallows, her face inclined downward as she searched the water at her feet.

"Oh dear, oh dear," she said, her hands pressed to her temples.

"What is the matter?" Njambi asked the woman.

"I have dropped my water pot into the river and without it I cannot carry water back to my family."

"Oh, that is terrible," Njambi said. She jumped down from the riverbank and began to help the woman. She was surprised when her hands touched something under the water that was not a rock, a log, or a tortoise. She lifted it up.

"My water pot!" the woman exclaimed. "You have found it. Many blessings upon you!"

Njambi said good-bye and began to cross the river, as this place looked to be as good as any to try to ford. The water grew deeper as she walked, surrounding her ankles, her knees, and her waist. The current grew stronger. It was hard for Njambi, the smallest of all her sisters, to fight the pull of the river. She felt her feet slipping in the mud. Just as the current was about to sweep her away, something long and slithery wrapped itself around her waist.

"Oh no, it is the python that tried to eat Wanjiku!" she screamed, feeling the thick body coil around her. "I will be swallowed whole!"

The snake-thing wrapped itself around her more tightly. Njambi was too small to fight. She felt herself ready to cry, not out of fear, but from the thought that she would never see her family again and that she had let her parents down. But just when she had lost all hope, she rose up and out of the water. She was lifted and hung suspended in the air, the water glittering as it passed beneath her. A fish jumped on the surface, dazzling her eyes. Njambi was not drowning. She was being carried across the river. It was not a snake that had snared her but a mother elephant that had gone for a swim with her baby. The mother elephant set Njambi down gently on the opposite bank while the baby let out a playful spray of water from its trunk.

"Thank you very much," Njambi said.

The elephant waved her trunk and lumbered back into the river to watch over her baby. Njambi looked across the river to see if the woman with the pot had witnessed the strange event, but she was gone.

The desert loomed ahead for Njambi, a flat, boiling sandscape with rippling dunes, shimmering light, and the dried, bleached bones of animals. These were animals who had become lost and died between the hammer of the sun and the anvil of the hardpan. Njambi was glad to have her calabash, as well as her kikoi, which she placed over her head to shield herself from the sun.

After a few miles, she came across an old man seated at the base of a dune. His gnarled hands were wrapped around a walking stick.

"Hello, sir," she said respectfully, remembering how to address her elders.

"Young lady," the old man said in a raspy voice, "My throat is very dry. Can you spare me some water?"

"I have some water in my gourd. I can share a little with you, but the rest I need, for I must cross the desert myself."

"You are a kind young lady," the man said, taking a small sip from her calabash. "Thank you very much for your generosity!"

She looked around and saw no one and no *thing* for as far as the eye could see. Njambi asked, "Sir, what are you doing out here in the desert, all alone? Aren't you afraid of being lost?"

The man smiled. He had dark eyes under droopy lids, but they had a twinkle to them that Njambi liked. "Sometimes *lost* is exactly where a person needs to be," he said.

"That doesn't make sense to me," Njambi said. She was young, and little, but thought of herself as very practical.

"It doesn't? Then what 'makes sense' to you, young lady?"

"Well, no one should get lost. You should always know where you are going, how many kilometers you have come and how many you have to go."

"And how do you know how many kilometers?"

"You count them, of course."

"But not everything that counts can be counted."

Njambi didn't say anything next. She realized that the man, like Dr. Chege, spoke in riddles, and she wondered if he too was a shaman, perhaps on a spirit journey of some sort. As the silence drew out he said, "The words *silent* and *listen* are spelled with the same letters, at least in English . . . Isn't that interesting?"

"Yes, sir, very interesting. But . . . sir, do you *like* being lost?"

"Aha, yes, I do. For only when lost can you truly find yourself. One must be defeated in order to be rescued."

"But that . . . that is the opposite of what—"

"Truth is a paradox, young lady. To keep a thing, we must give it away. To hold a thing, one must keep an open hand. To get help, one must give it.

"You speak in riddles, sir. Are you a shaman?"

The old man shook his head, flexing and adjusting his fingers on his staff. "I'm just a wanderer, turning things inside out and upside down as I walk about and reflect."

"That . . . is interesting . . ." Njambi said, because she was not sure what to say next. Old men and their riddles had not been particularly helpful to her as of late, nor had they brought much good news. She looked across the wastes and through the shimmering air at Mount Kaliande. But it appeared the old man was not done speaking.

"Dear girl, even a potter must create emptiness—a hollow in a pot—in order for there to ever be fullness."

Another paradox, but Njambi was beginning to see some sense in his words.

"I guess you are right. I had never looked at it that way."

"Excellent," the old man said, rising and stretching his legs. Njambi realized he was very tall, like a Dinka or a Maasai. "Well, don't let me delay you any longer. Safe journey, little one. Thank you for sharing your water."

"Yes, thank you, sir. I wish you a safe journey, too."

The man climbed the nearest dune and was gone. Njambi continued. As she crossed the dunes and wandered along the *wadis*, she came across more skeletons of animals that had become lost and died. "I hope I do not end up like them," she said. But as the sun grew higher, it burned her skin and made her eyes water. The sand scorched her feet, making walking painful. She drank some water from her calabash, but it soon was empty. After many kilometers, her mouth grew quite dry. Her tongue felt like it was made of cotton, and her eyelids stuck together when she blinked. It was as if her eyes and her mouth were covered in glue. Just when she thought she could continue no further, clouds rolled into the sky and blocked the sun. A soft rain fell. It soothed Njambi's skin, refilled her calabash, and also cooled the sand, making it more pleasant to walk upon. A refreshing breeze followed, carrying the scents of desert flowers. She was struck with the stark beauty that surrounded her.

"The desert can actually be quite beautiful and serene," Njambi said to herself.

The desert ended at the foot of Mount Kaliande. Once, long ago, it had been a fiery volcano, but now it slept with a snow-covered brow. It was huge, its sides rising to their own horizons. Its immensity reminded Njambi of a small planet, come to rest on this seam of the Earth that was the Rift Valley. Somewhere on Mount Kaliande's slopes, hidden within its fissures was the spring that held the Water of Life. But Njambi did not know where to begin searching for it. The mountain was so large, and she was just the littlest daughter.

"Oh, how will I ever find the spring?" she cried, beginning to despair.

"I know where to find the spring you speak of," an old woman said. She was dressed in a burgundy wrap with the plaid designs popular among the Maasai tribe. She sat hunched over beneath a jacaranda tree, its blossoms floating down around her like a lavender snow. Njambi had not noticed her at first and was startled by her appearance. But Njambi quickly composed herself. The old woman continued, "I would like to go to the spring myself, but I cannot climb the mountain without help."

"Madam," Njambi said, remembering the way to address an old woman, "I will help you climb if you show me the way!"

"Very well. Let us climb together," the woman said.

Njambi and the old woman started off side by side, Njambi holding the woman's hand and letting her lean upon her shoulder when she needed support. At first, the mountain slopes were lush and covered with acacia trees, elephant trunk flowers, and hedges of clematis. After a while, the woody trees were replaced by bamboo reeds. Buffalo grazed around them, slowly munching grass while hyraxes scurried away for cover. Bush babies watched them from the shadows under the bamboo canopies, their eerie glowing eyes tracking their every move.

"The mountain slopes contain their own climates, each like their own world as the ground grows higher and the air colder," the old woman said.

Njambi saw what she meant. After a day of climbing up through forests of whispering trees, they passed into cloudy moorlands. Here the ground was covered in coarse heather. Strange, alien-like trees Njambi had never seen before rose up out of the gloom. The woman called them giant lobelias. They resembled green clubs. Then there were the even stranger groundsel trees, topped with antennae of daisy-like flowers and rings of palm fronds, their sides protected by an armor of dead scales.

Njambi and the woman spent the night in the shelter of some rocks and ate a few bananas the woman had carried with her from lower elevations. The next day, as they climbed higher, the land turned to tundra, the heather growing thin. It was replaced by lichen and moss with the occasional aster, their stems lined with long silver hairs for capturing warmth and water. The wind blew moss balls about the travelers' feet, like miniature tumbleweeds.

The air grew as cold as winter—colder than Njambi had ever experienced, much less imagined. As they climbed higher, something strange seemed to be happening to the woman: each time Njambi looked at her, she seemed younger.

*I thought she had more wrinkles on her face,* Njambi thought. Later, she was sure the woman's back had become straighter than it had been at the bottom of the mountain. "The thin air must be getting to me," Njambi said to herself.

They continued to climb for another day. The grass disappeared altogether, and they wandered through a wasteland of jagged rocks with shattered faces and razor edges. The wind grew fierce, a cold knife against Njambi's skin, howling down from the snowy cap of the mountain. The wind spoke with a voice of loneliness. Pinnacles of hardened lava rose around them. Here the landscape spoke of ancient eruptions, heaving earth, and the gradual wearing down of rock by rain and wind, snow and ice. Gone were the birds of tropical and temperate climes; the ibises, the bulbuls, and the boubous were nowhere to be seen or heard. Here only the harsh cries of gold and black lammergeyers cascaded down the rocky sides. They were giant birds, with wide wingspans adapted to the thin air and well-insulated plumage that looked more like fur than feathers.

Njambi felt the change in the air. She had to take three, even four breaths, where before she had only taken one. The cold, dry air made her lungs ache, and her skin was lined with white cracks. Her heart was working extra hard in her chest. She grew tired and stumbled in the loose shale, cutting herself on the sharp volcanic stones. Each step became a greater effort for her. Now Njambi felt like she was leaning on the old woman.

As Njambi grew weaker, a second strange thing happened: the woman stepped ahead of her and began to lead her by the hand. But she was clearly no longer an old woman. She was young, tall, and strong. She strode with long legs and took confident steps. The cold did not affect her.

"I think I am imagining things that are not real," Njambi muttered. "This must be altitude sickness. I should turn back."

But she could not bear the thought of failing her family, so she trudged upward, holding the woman's hand.

They reached a point so high that Njambi felt she could almost touch the stars peeking out overhead. Snow was piled in banks on either side of their path and crunched underneath their feet. Njambi's breath wreathed about her head. She shivered and shook. The woman, definitely leading and definitely appearing younger, like a fit Olympic athlete, led them down into a fissure and into an ice cave. Its sides were shades of amethyst and beryl, shot through with white veins of crystal snow. The air, by contrast, was warm and humid, the sides dripping with water droplets that fell, chiming, into a pool. The water in the pool was so warm that steam rose from its surface and made the air thick and cloudy. The change was too much for Njambi. She loosened her wrap to cool herself, for she was suddenly sweating as if in a sauna, and sat lest she faint.

Through the mist, Njambi could just make out a few stone walls. They were painted with pictures of dancing figures with the long, stylized masks characteristic of pictures she had seen of West African masquerade ceremonies. Something about them was full of beauty and foreboding all at once . . . the way Njambi imagined people were supposed to feel when before a supernatural being. One figure was more compelling than the others: his long black-and-red face could have been laughing, or it could have been screeching, the mouth opening with long white fangs, ready to devour her soul.

Even though she was no longer cold, Njambi shivered looking into his burning blue irises, the bottomless pupils eclipsing them like black moons. The shifting of mist made the demon's fangs move, as if they were closing in on her. For a moment she was certain the figure *would* step out of the rock, cross the pool, and swallow her.

The woman stopped and turned in place, drawing Njambi's attention back to her. The former crone now stood tall and grand next to the pool. There was no doubt that she had transformed into a younger woman. She opened her arms and spoke in a melodious voice, "Behold, the Water of Life!"

"Who are you?" Njambi asked. "How can this be?"

The woman smiled brightly. "I am Ife, the spirit of life. This is my pool and my mountain."

Njambi quickly shifted to get down on her knees, realizing she was in front of a goddess. Ife spoke again, but this time her voice was kind and generous.

"Sweet Njambi, rise. Do not cast your face to the ground. Yes, be humble, for you are made of earth, but also be noble, for you are made of stars."

Njambi looked up from under the kikoi she had used to cover her face. Her hands were shaking. "I still don't understand."

"It is my duty to guard the Water of Life. Only those who pass three tests of the heart can be led to it."

"What are the tests I must pass?" Njambi asked weakly. "I am very tired. Will I be allowed to rest first?"

Ife laughed. "You have already passed them, my child."

Njambi looked to the side and, to her surprise, saw the boy from the forest, the woman from the river, and the old man from the desert standing on the other side of the pool.

"Now I *know* the thin air is making me see things," Njambi said.

"Your eyes do not deceive," Ife said. "This is Msitu," she said, pointing to the boy, "Spirit of the forest. When you helped him, you gained passage through the forest." Then she turned to the woman. "This is Mto, spirit of the river. When you found her pot, she made sure you crossed the river safely." Ife turned to the old man. "And this old man is Jangwa, the wise spirit of the desert. In exchange for a sip of your water, he granted you comfortable passage across the scorching wastes."

Njambi felt overwhelmed. She bowed her head, placed her hands on her heart, and thanked the spirits many times.

"Now fill your bottle with the water from the spring," Ife said. "You will have to hurry back home, for your father has little time left."

"But it is such a long way," Njambi said. "It will take me days to return."

"Don't worry, Njambi," Mto said. "We are here to help you."

"As you helped us," Jangwa said, filling up Njambi's bottle for her.

Msitu danced over the rocks and ice, his bare feet unaffected by the sharp edges and cold, slick surfaces. He paused before the mouth of the ice cave, where he whistled. A sharp cry answered, and one of the huge gold and black lammergeyers swooped into their midst and perched next to Njambi, its wings stirring up the clouds of steam. Up close, she could see it was a bizarre looking bird, as if the parts of a hawk and a condor had been put together under a coat of gold and black fur.

"This is Akinyi. He will help you reach home in time," Msitu said.

"But how?"

"Like this," Ife said. She waved her hand and snapped her fingers with a loud crack. Akinyi let out a cry, flapping up a small windstorm with his wings before taking Njambi up in his talons and soaring out into the starry night.

Njambi let out a yelp of fright and grabbed a tight hold of Akinyi's legs. The ground fell away with the slope of the mountain. Njambi's head spun with vertigo. Then her stomach felt as if it flipped inside her as Akinyi dove downward. Moving at such speed, Njambi felt the temperature grow warmer in passing bands of thickening air. What had taken days to climb, now took only moments to descend, as if Akinyi could bend time and space with the beat of his wings. Soon they were soaring over the desert wastes, the sinuous lines of dunes and variegated colors of the crystal sands flowing like the dancing brush strokes of a painting.

Next they crossed the ribbon that was the River Kaliande, which Njambi now knew was fed by the ice and snow of the mountain, as well as the gentle seasonal rains that swept down its slopes as if on the very wishes of old man Jangwa. The dense forest and its emerald canopy passed in the space beyond Njambi's feet. It was wondrous and strange to see the tops of trees below her toes. Akinyi leaned his wings into the wind, turning on the tips of his feathers. He homed in on Njambi's village and her family's house, and they plunged like a well-aimed arrow at its target. As they passed over houses with a "WHOOSH," Akinyi let out a loud cry, and the neighbors pointed and shouted. There was quite a crowd and a commotion as Akinyi circled their home then set Njambi down. She did not even stop, but rather landed running, quickly entering their hut and calling out to her parents.

She found her mother at her father's side. Murito's skin was grayish, and his lips trembled without sound as he tried to speak. All of Njambi's sisters had returned to stand in vigil, for they expected their father to pass and now were remorseful they had shown so much selfishness before. Njambi burst past them, pushing her way in, and climbed to her father's side. She handed him the bottle to drink. After a few sips, in the space of moments, Murito's color returned, his flesh filled out. His voice became strong again and his eyes bright.

"Oh, Njambi, my littlest daughter, you have succeeded in the impossible!" Murito cried out, tears wetting his face. He picked her up and danced with her, holding her up over his head.

The entire family wept with joy. The neighbors heard the story and soon the entire village and the surrounding community were talking about the wonders that Njambi, the Littlest Daughter, had accomplished.

"I could not have done it without help or the spirit of helping," Njambi said.

After that day, Njambi was no longer ignored by her sisters. They actually looked to her for advice and example. People called Njambi wise, saying that her contact with the spirit world had given her knowledge and insights. Njambi was not as sure. She felt those insights were full of contradictions: the Water of Life existed, but one had to climb into a dreadful wasteland to get it. The spring and its pool were hot with the vitality of life but surrounded by cold darkness and thin air that threatened only death. Even Ife herself lived in the looming shadow of terrible things, the threatening columns of lava, the stones sharp as fangs, and that fierce god who had stared at her from the painted cave wall. Njambi still sometimes saw that red and black face in her dreams, his name unknown, his nature still a mystery.

But in her dreams she also felt the exhilaration of Akinyi's flight and recalled the coolness of the soothing desert rains and the fragrance of flowers opening under them. Njambi still puzzled over all the mysteries she had glimpsed in the riddles of the spirits and in her experience at the edge of their world. She felt, if anything, they had turned her perspective inside out and upside down, a bit like Jangwa sought to do on his walkabouts: to get help, you had to give it; to keep something, you had to give it away; to be found, you had to be lost. She did not profess to have any answers to these paradoxes.

When things felt too heavy and complicated, she would reflect at last on Dr. Chege's words: life was short and not permanent. *Spoken only the way a doctor-shaman could,* she half-laughed, half-grumbled to herself. She knew there was more truth in these words than ever before, for she had glimpsed something eternal up on Mount Kaliande. Njambi could sense that life was a passage between one world and the next, darkness to light and to darkness again, and then, who knew? Most days, understanding felt just beyond her comprehension. Instead of being frustrated, she tried not to take it, or herself, too seriously.

Instead Njambi would wander outside. Her feet on the earth, her eyes cast to the starry sky, the questions and mysteries would fall away. She would feel big and little at once, and she would know, for that moment, she was exactly where she needed to be.

# ~ Part 3 ~

# How to Fight Zombies

President Ajuma Wukumbo had called upon the army, the police forces, and all the country's civil engineers to construct a perimeter around the capital. Her ministers had enacted a curfew to protect the citizenry who had not yet been infected by the zombie outbreak.

But still, the zombies only multiplied. The scourge had begun in the countryside. Reports had come in from far-flung villages of bodies rising up from the grave, wandering about at night, shambling on decomposing limbs and broken bones, barging into huts and homes, drawn inexorably on by the scent of living flesh. A single bite from them would lead to fevers, chills, and a discoloration of skin, followed by a coma and even a deathlike state. But that was not the end. The newly bit would transform, their bodies having turned a shade of gray-blue. They would "wake," ravenous to feast upon living flesh themselves. With their bodies not yet decayed, these new zombies were faster than their revenant counterparts (called shamblers). Nimble and agile, these newly infected (referred to as runners) presented an even greater menace to the living. Yet except for their empty white eyes and their discolored flesh, they still resembled the deceased people they had once been, so no one was prepared to hurt or harm them. Some families tried to keep them captive, until a cure could be found. But whatever bindings or locked rooms they were confined by, they always escaped, leading to disastrous consequences.

The Ministry of Health insisted that this zombie plague was not caused by black magic, but rather a virus. Doctors and scientists were hard at work, day and night, trying to develop a vaccine. The last thing the populace should do was panic. After all, the army, the police, and civil engineers were maintaining the perimeter around the city and its environs. They set up roadblocks of riot shields and electric fences usually reserved for keeping lions and leopards away from farmers' herds of cattle. The nightly news showed officers and soldiers alike standing guard, stoic in their resolve and faithful in their duty (at least that was what the news reporters said). Even as the hordes of shamblers and runners pressed up against the barriers, the message from one government spokesperson after another was the same:

Don't panic. All is under control.

And yet, by word of mouth, there were always rumors. Rumors of places where the ministry had been forced to pull the perimeter back; rumors of runners that had slipped through to be found in someone's basement or in their garden, where the creatures would jump out and attack. . .

The government denied any such breaches, but the sight of Ministry of Health vans and Ministry of Security troop carriers speeding down neighborhood streets to surround a home then cordon it off with lines of police tape, plastic sheeting, and biohazard signs told a different story.

It did not help matters that President Wukumbo had not been seen or even appeared on camera for weeks, locked away in the statehouse as she was. She was working to find a solution to the crisis. That was the official word. But rumors flew here too: the president had fled the country on a secret flight to South Africa, or she had even succumbed to the virus herself and was undergoing experimental treatment in Saudi Arabia, or even worse, she had been bit and she herself had become a zombie, running rampant in the confines of the presidential compound, her aides doing their best to keep her condition secret.

All the while, the number of zombies, shamblers and runners, grew. The news cameras on television and amateur footage on the internet revealed more and more ghastly faces pressing up against the barriers, clawing up walls, struggling to squeeze through fences, even as more filled every street and lane and feeder road to the horizon.

Don't panic. All is under control.

These remained the official words from every government ministry. It was the message from guards stationed at border crossings into the neighboring countries, even as they locked down the gates and pointed their weapons at anyone who tried to leave. It was the uniform stance of the international community, even though they had voted unanimously at the UN to quarantine the entire country . . . indefinitely.

And it was what Anastasia and Paulo's parents told them whenever they prepared to leave the house to make a trip to the hypermarket for supplies. For the survivors of the epidemic, trapped in the capital city, it was considered patriotic to continue with daily life, to persevere as if nothing was out of the ordinary. The Ministry of Education kept schools within the perimeter in session, and the hypermarkets had been ordered to remain open, although they had to comply with the government rationing requirements. This prevented bank runs and price gouging, and kept the shelves from being stripped bare by panic purchasing. And yet, people mumbled under their breath, in close quarters, behind closed doors. They admitted their anxiety about the food running out, for fewer and fewer supply trucks were able to get through the horde and safely to the barriers. They wondered if the perimeter would hold. They made plans for what to do if . . . *when* . . . the zombies broke through, where they would go, how they would flee, with whom. . .

Don't panic. All is under control.

That was still the official word on the radio when some of the schools began to close, despite the decrees from the Ministry of Education. Anastasia remembered the day hers did. They were in geometry class when a scream startled everyone. Students and teacher turned to the window where they saw Mrs. Oworo, the health and biology teacher, running, holding up her skirt, her face contorted in sheer terror as a running zombie chased after her. She was saved only by the quickness of the groundskeeper and the headmaster, who, at great risk to their own lives, tackled the zombie and tied it up. Even bound and restrained with thick ropes, the zombie thrashed and writhed, snapping its teeth to catch a bite of living flesh. When one of the children recognized the zombie as Mr. Singe, the kindly Indian man who sold them chapatis, chai, and curry chicken from the kiosk across the road, the headmaster decided to close the school until further notice. A second shuffling zombie was spotted rummaging through the rubbish bin later that day. No one recognized the victim from around the neighborhood, so it was thought that this second zombie was one that had slipped in through the perimeter, although some people still refused to believe it could even happen, and some parents still thought the school had a patriotic duty to remain open. But the headmaster was adamant and sent a regretful letter home to parents informing them that he and the staff could no longer guarantee the safety of the children.

Don't panic. All is under control.

It was what Anastasia and Paulo's parents repeated that very Saturday morning . . . or was it Friday? Anastasia had lost track. Without school and without being able to leave the house—for the curfew did not allow children outside in public even during the day without proper supervision—one day just looked like every other. Anastasia wasn't panicked herself, or worried, as much as she was bored. It was house arrest as far as she was concerned. The television was a monotonous bore: more news stories on zombies or reruns of game shows and reality TV. The other channels were only showing happy films to cheer people up: Bollywood films, Disney movies from the 80s and 90s, Pixar flicks, but no Nollywood films—those were too full of drama, conflict, and some stories even featured plotlines with juju, which government censors thought might just add to peoples' worries.

So Nollywood was out. So was Big Brother Africa, Survivor, or any other reality shows that featured people stuck in houses or on islands together trying to get along (or not) . . . *that* was too close to reality.

"Watch your brother while we are out," Anastasia's mother said, kissing her and Paulo on their heads before she left with their father for the grocery run.

"Ok, Mum," Anastasia said from the couch. She didn't look up to meet her mother's warm, almond-shaped eyes, as she was deeply engrossed in her phone. She had downloaded the latest game that was all the rage in the country that week: Zombie Killers— Africa Edition, and was playing with her friends, who were also all on lockdown, all hopelessly bored, and tired of it all. They griped through Anastasia's earbuds while their avatars chopped off zombie limbs with machetes or bashed their heads with cricket bats or hammers, the points of each kill rising up from the bloody remains like the souls zombies didn't have.

Anastasia's avatar stalked into a room along with her friends, Alba, Winnie, and James. Alba's character, a tall fierce warrior queen with long braids and bare arms clasped in gold bangles, drew back a bow and fired an arrow into a zombie creeping up on Winnie's sorceress, clad resplendently in her white robe.

"Thanks," Winnie's voice sounded from the left earbud.

"Anytime," Alba said in the right.

"Don't let your guard down. I think the level boss is in the next room," James said. Anastasia could hear him chomping gum in her ear.

"Ewww, gross. That is so annoying, James. Spit your gum out," Alba said.

"Sorry, I get nervous," James said. "It helps me concentrate. Whoa, here he comes."

The level boss came charging through a wall and into their midst: a mutated, two-headed zombie elephant complete with four tusks and two trunks. It would be a handful. As they were coordinating their attack and dodging an ambush of zombie minions from just outside the frame of the screen, Paulo tugged on Anastasia's trouser leg. Her brother was sitting at the other end of the couch watching television. He had flipped through the channels to land on a news station. *Another* reporter was interviewing *another* police captain—or was it an army captain? They all looked the same now, sharing uniforms and body armor. And they all look fatigued with red, sleepless eyes and ever-leaner faces, due to the diminishing rations. This officer offered the same old drivel about "working day and night to maintain vigilance while the MoH developed a cure" . . .blah . . . blah . . . blah.

"Sia, do you think they will find a cure soon?" Paulo asked.

"Sure," Anastasia said, whacking off the head of a zombie minion and dodging a fireball from the trunk of the elephant.

"When?" Paulo asked, peering up over her phone now.

"At your six, Winnie." Anastasia wheeled around to slice another zombie in half at the waist. "Not now, Paulo."

"What's that?" James asked.

"Nothing, just my annoying brother."

"Stay focused," James said.

"I *am* focused. Alba, we need your arrows over here."

"Got it."

"Winnie, go for the boss. It's going to take magic. I got you covered from the zombie squirrels," James said.

"Ugh, they are so gross. Look at the splatter," Winnie said as one of the squirrels got flattened by James's mallet.

"You can tell this was developed by American or European gamers. There are no squirrels in Africa. There should be monkeys or something instead," Anastasia said.

"Good point," Alba said, firing a fusillade of arrows.

"Focus, team!" James said.

The elephant moved upon them, closing off their room to maneuver.

"I can't get the angle with the arrows," Alba said.

"I got you." Winne's sorceress sent over a flux of magic that cleared the space around Alba.

"No, Winnie, focus on the boss," James said.

"God, James, you are so bossy—"

"No, he's right. Even if he chews gum like a cow on quat," Anastasia said. "You've got the best weapon to take him out."

"They're saying that the police are pulling back the perimeter in Greenfield Estates and Yaya Market," Paulo interrupted Anastasia again, his eyes wide with alarm.

"Paulo, not now!" Anastasia said.

"But—"

"Sia, Sia, we need you."

"I'm here, I'm here," Anastasia said, jamming in her earbud and jumping off the couch. This was too critical a moment to be distracted by her dumb brother.

"Sia, why are you breathing in my ear like that?" Winnie asked.

"I'm running upstairs to get away from my brother. He is such a troll," Anastasia said, slamming the door to her room and throwing herself across her bed.

"I've got bottom of the screen," Alba said.

"South," James said, a stickler for cardinal directions when playing. "Your bottom is not my bottom."

"I'll say."

"Whatever."

"Winnie, get in position. Do your thing."

"Roger."

Winnie leapt into the air to land facing down the two elephant heads. Before they could rip her apart with their serrated tusks, Winnie blasted out an aura of spells, one pulse after another. The elephant shook, hit points rising up over it, tallying to their team score. The dead flesh of the elephant dropped off, exposing bones, musculature, and empty hollows.

"All right!" James said.

"Hold on, check this out," Winne said. Anastasia could hear the smile in her voice. Her sorceress spun in a circle like a dancer, her robes expanding like a flower in bloom. A tight spiral of light enveloped her for an instant before expanding out into a hurricane, its power passing safely over her teammates but obliterating the squirrels, the minions, and finally shattering the elephant into clumps of smoking flesh and stringy entrails.

"Whoa."

"That was some finishing move."

"Gross."

"Awesome."

The hit points continued to tally up. Anastasia could hear the others shifting out of their seats, running to the fridge for food or drinks while the next level loaded. Anastasia rolled on her back and stared up at the ceiling, where her glow-in-the-dark stars were stuck on the plaster, yellow-green and boring in the light of day.

"We rock," James said.

"We ought to, this is all we do anymore," Winnie said, over the sound of her unwrapping a snack of some kind.

"I heard they were going to be shifting all the school lessons to online teaching," Alba said.

"Ugh, so boring. I'm tired of being inside," Alba said.

"Me too," Anastasia added.

James was silent, unnaturally so, which meant he was probably on mute, which also meant he was likely taking a pee. Anastasia would hold off asking him for his opinion. "I miss going out to school," she said. "At this rate, we won't ever graduate to go to university."

"I heard the perimeter is falling back again," Winnie said around her food.

"Yeah, Paulo said something to me about Greenfield and Yaya Market."

"Not just there, but Githare and Maribella Estates too," Alba said.

"Really?"

"Yeah, they just didn't want to announce that too, because they don't want people to panic."

"Don't panic. All is under control," Anastasia mocked in an officious voice.

Background noise from the radio and the voices of James's brothers and sisters cut back in as James unmuted himself. "Those are just rumors," he said.

"James, I hope you washed your hands," Winnie giggled.

"Those rumors have a way of being true," Alba said.

"My neighbor's house just got cordoned off and quarantined night before last. We haven't heard from them since," Winnie said.

"No way."

They were all silent a while, the download circle pinwheeling on the screen amid their avatar profile pictures, looking by turns fierce, serene, and noble, belying the anxiety Anastasia knew they all were suddenly feeling. The real world was intruding on their virtual one. James was eager to retreat back into fantasy, immediately yammering on about what to expect on the next level. Anastasia thought of Paulo, those normally eager eyes of his instead filled with alarm.

"The next level has ghosts in it," James said, chewing gum again.

"James, really?" Alba's voice was exasperated.

"Yeah, ghosts. I mean, the developers need to pick a lane, right? Is this a fantasy game or sci-fi? You can't have both; it doesn't make sense."

"No James, I meant the gum."

"That's what you two are talking about, when we could be the next zombies, in real life?" Winnie scolded.

"It's not worth worrying about. The government says it's under control," James said.

"I don't know. No one has seen President Wukumbo in weeks. You think she's infected?" Anastasia asked.

"I think we will need more magic on the next level, because I don't know if Alba's arrows are going to affect the ghosts."

"Ugh, James," Anastasia rolled her eyes.

"Come on, we all know the President left on a private jet and is hiding out at some fancy resort in the Seychelles until this blows over," James said.

"It does make you wonder though, regarding your first remark, James," Winnie said.

"The one about rumors?"

"No, the one about fantasy and sci-fi. I mean, if there are such things as zombies in real life these days, why not ghosts?"

"Well, I know there are both in this game and the level is ninety percent finished loading."

*Real life.* Anastasia slid her eyes from the screen and took in her room. The colors were muted compared to the graphics of the game, even on her most outrageous posters and magazine cutouts. Clothes, some dirty, some clean and in need of folding, were scattered about. Her school uniform hung on a hanger, pressed and ready but sadly unused for weeks. Her laptop with all its stickers was closed, and her school textbooks and notebooks were growing fuzzy with dust.

What was real life? A mess. And here they were, disappearing into a game of pixels and techno music, while advertisements flashed at them at the bottom of the screen. Anastasia rolled over, one of her earbuds falling out. She was suddenly, uncomfortably aware of the quiet in her house. It extended even to the street outside. There were no cars, no voices of people in the lanes between, no hawking of sellers. Not even the *thwock-thwock* of a helicopter or the distant roar of a jet plane. She couldn't see or hear the zombie hordes, but she could feel them in the oppressive silence, the sense of being trapped in an ever-shrinking space. She wished her parents were home already.

"Hey all, I need to sign off."

"You all right, Anastasia?" Winnie asked.

"Yeah, I just think I should check on my brother."

"We're at ninety-five percent."

"I'll be back soon, James. The beginning of the level is always the easiest."

"Your funeral."

"Whatever. BRB."

"Bye, Sia!"

"Later."

"See ya."

Anastasia signed off, closed the app, and called out for Paulo, yelling his name loud enough that he would hear her through her door. When he didn't respond, she immediately felt annoyed. A second before it had felt like he was dying for her to talk to him, now he wasn't even paying attention.

*Figures.*

She yanked out the other earbud, threw her phone down onto the bed, and slipped her feet back into her house sandals. When she opened the door and started downstairs, her sandals slapped loudly in the stairwell. She called out again, imagining her brother zoned out in front of the television.

"Paulo, what are you doing?"

Still no answer. She turned down the hall, her footsteps echoing in the empty kitchen and the quiet dining room. When she turned into the living room, she saw the couch was empty. The television was still on, but the volume was low, so she wasn't sure why Paulo had not heard her.

The lights were on, and the television had been switched to a channel playing the *Lion King.* She rolled her eyes, picked up the remote and clicked it off.

"Paulo."

Still nothing. The couch cushions still held the shape of her brother where he had been seated. She felt as if he were still present, maybe just lurking behind the couch, ready to scare her. She preempted him by leaping onto the cushions and leaning over the wicker back of the couch with a loud, "GYYAAAAAAHHH!"

But Paulo was not there either. She saw nothing but empty space and the flat of the floor between the couch back and the wall. It was where Paulo always liked to hide, but perhaps he was trying to change things up. She checked behind their father's favorite chair in the corner, but he was not hiding there either.

"Come on Paulo, I don't feel like playing hide-and-seek right now. Mum and Dad will be angry if I tell them you were hiding from me." Anastasia knew they were much more likely to be angry at her for not watching her brother more closely, but she was not about to admit that and lose leverage over him.

She checked the dining room, the kitchen pantry, the laundry room, and all the downstairs closets. She even went back upstairs to look in his room, then in the upstairs closets, then their father and mother's study, which they were not allowed to enter. She peeked in the door. "Paulo if you are in here, you are in big trouble."

But he wasn't.

*If he's gone outside without me, I'll make sure Mum and Dad give him such a beating . . .*

Their yard had a wall and grounds that were the envy of the neighborhood. This was thanks to their gardener, Peter Motinda. He was an older, blind man but he somehow kept the bushes trimmed neatly and the flowers flourishing year-round. The vegetables and tubers he grew were fecund miracles. He had even managed to bring on young blind children and youth to mentor as apprentices, teaching them how to live and perceive the world through their other senses.

Anastasia loved the garden, and it was safe—mostly. But Paulo was definitely not allowed outside to play in it without her. Now her fury at his disobedience was brewing over, and she slapped the door outside open, noting that it had been left unlocked.

*He definitely came through here . . . and didn't even lock the door. I'll kill him.*

Their garden walls were high, as were the walls around their front courtyard. Their neighbors on either side of them were vigilant, but with stories of running zombies scaling walls around the city, she knew they could not be too careful.

"Paulo!"

She ran down the passageway between the house and the wall separating them from the neighbor's lot, grateful when she stepped into the wider space of the back garden. The garden was terraced, three levels sloping down with a variety of stonework, wicker lawn furniture, and an open green lawn for football or badminton. Lattice canopies, shady with vines of bougainvillea, stretched over the walkways and sitting areas. There was even a Japanese rock garden. It took the place of a fountain or pool—those were out of the question, since they were breeding havens for mosquitos and thus malaria. Although Anastasia still felt short with her brother, she could not help but feel a little sense of peace creep into her, shifting her ire to a lighter shade of irritation. It was the magic of Peter's green spaces. She decided she would not beat Paulo herself and didn't want her parents to beat him either, but she would sure give him a stern scolding.

But first she had to find him.

"Paulo!"

No answer. But as she descended down to the second terrace, something else caught her eye: footprints straight across the carefully raked sands of the Japanese rock garden. The lines in the sand were smooth and perfect, without blemish, wobble, or sharp edges. They radiated like ripples in a pond from the stones that sat with the immobile presence of deep thoughts. The arrangements and features were always all the more striking considering their gardener's blindness.

But now some idiot, maybe her brother, had walked across them. Without giving it too much more thought as to whom, Anastasia ran down the third set of stone steps into the lowest bit of the garden. This section had a shady trellis, as well as an open swath of lawn they used for games. It was here that Anastasia spotted the interloper. He was a kid. By his size likely between her age of thirteen and Paulo's nine. The intruder's back was turned, but Anastasia knew much about him already by his khaki-colored safari jacket, matching cargo pants, and even a pith helmet, like a 19th century safari hunter.

A tourist. And likely an American at that. He was clearly lost, having wandered away from whatever hotel he was trapped in because of the cancelled international flights—although Anastasia had imagined that the quarantine of her country would have just been for *her* people—foreigners with their money, connections, and simple sense of entitlement often seemed to find ways around the rules imposed on them by a "third world," "developing" country.

Anastasia rolled her eyes hard for the second time that morning. The tourist boy's credentials were made all the more obvious by the beaded Maasai-themed camera strap around his neck—he had probably been charged an outrageous tourist price for it too, but Anastasia never had any sympathy for whites who were charged more for items she and other locals would pay a tenth of the price for. She thought of it as a white-privilege tax. They could afford it, so be it.

The boy was hunched over, eating something. She couldn't see what, but she could hear the munching and slobbering. She imagined his face, even before she saw it, as rotund, sunburned, smeared with chocolate—sadly this was the stereotype she and her friends held for most Americans. She circled, taking in his get up, the pockets down the pant legs, the pouches on the vest, the leopard print on the seams and cuffs.

*Do they even know what parodies they make of themselves?*

"Excuse me, but you are on private property—" she began to say.

The boy grunted and whipped around with preternatural speed. Something flew off from his face, a bit of melted chocolate perhaps? It didn't take long for Anastasia to realize she had made a grave mistake. The boy's face was not smeared with chocolate but with blood. His skin was an alabaster shade of white with patches of gray. His eyes, opened wide like a frightened animal, were bluish-white. But the most horrifying aspect was not even his appearance, but rather what—who—he was eating.

Paulo.

Her brother lay semiconscious, his clothes disheveled and dirty, his hair full of dried grass and leaves, as if he had struggled with the zombie of the white American boy before being dragged down to this place where, no longer able to wait, the zombie boy had taken a bite of Paulo's shoulder.

The boy stalked closer to Anastasia. How she wished she had not left her phone on her bed. The boy rolled his tongue around his mouth, lapping up her brother's blood. She had to do something, but she wasn't sure what. She could run, leading the zombie boy away, but she still needed to get her brother help. The boy took another step towards her, the broken telephoto lens of his camera looking at her like a lopsided eye. As a newly infected victim, his body was not dead or rotting. He would be able to pursue her with adrenaline-fueled speed and strength.

And zombie hunger.

Anastasia wanted to call for help, but her heart was stuck in her throat, her pulse pounding in her neck. If she cried out, would it provoke him or scare him? Was there a rock or stick she could use? Could she even make it to the steps, much less the house?

Paulo let out a soft groan. It distracted the zombie for a second, his face turning back towards his catch, his tongue flicking out.

Many things happened at once. Anastasia started forward, determined to knock the zombie down, grab her brother, and make a run for it. But just as she stepped forward, an equal force yanked backwards on her collar, pulling her in the opposite direction. A voice she knew well, Esmeralda, Peter the gardener's latest apprentice, spoke a soft but firm order in her ear.

"Wait." Esmeralda's voice was calm and steady. Did she not know there was a zombie there? She was also blind, but somehow she had snuck up behind Anastasia, without even the zombie noticing. "Just wait, Anastasia," she repeated.

At the same moment, Peter Motinda appeared in the side of Anastasia's vision, his body erect, his head tilted slightly back, his eyes closed, as if he were in a state of serene prayer. Only the twitch of his jaw betrayed his fierce concentration as he took in the scene with his other senses. The zombie was startled, his head wagging back and forth, his hands out to his sides like a skateboarder trying to regain his balance. It was just the hesitation Peter needed. He pulled his cane from his belt. It was the folding type that quickly snapped out to full length. He swung it, ninja-like at the zombie. He struck the boy's head, stunning him for a moment before the zombie belatedly put up his hands. Peter struck again, now at the boy's exposed sides, the cane swooshing through the air and cracking in loud slaps against the torso, the arms, and the back of the zombie. The boy spun in circles, not able to anticipate where the next lightning strike would come from. As if by a design Peter had already planned, the zombie began to retreat from Paulo, the gardener corralling him into the open, the small bloody hands raised and fingers curled like the claws of a cornered cat.

"Now, Esmeralda," Peter said.

The pressure around Anastasia's neck released and Esmeralda leapt past Anastasia, dancing around Paulo's inert body and playing out a length of rope, the end of which she threw out to Peter. He caught it, reaching his hand out to the side without needing to turn his head, as if he had known the rope would be in that precise point in space, at that precise point in time, all along. Then the two of them ran in opposite directions, circling the zombie, Peter walking in slow, measured steps clockwise, while Esmeralda moved counterclockwise, impossibly summersaulting over Peter's length of rope on each rotation, just before she would have otherwise tripped over it. Before the zombie could escape, they had him wrapped, once, twice, three times, and more, his whole body bound up like a little grub. With a yank, they tipped him over so that he fell facedown, growling and snarling, bound like an angry warthog, but unable to harm anyone further with his snapping jaws. Peter and Esmeralda had that bloody mouth of his gagged in short order.

The zombie subdued and Esmeralda standing guard over him, Peter moved to Paulo's side. Anastasia was already over her brother. He was sweating, his eyes fluttering while he murmured softly, as if crying out for help, lost in a great, distant nightmare.

"Is he bit?" Peter asked.

"Yes, on his shoulder. It looks bad, Peter. Will he be okay?"

Peter did not say so, only, "Let's get him into the house."

The house fell into chaos.

It was nothing short of a catastrophe, and Anastasia knew it was all her fault.

Her parents returned home shortly after they had carried Paulo into the house. Their panic was immediate and overwhelming, both of them distraught, manic in their worry for their son. The disaster was all consuming, but it was only the beginning. Anastasia's parents' fury at her was beyond description—literally, for neither could even find the words to confront her. Instead they glared at her in deep disappointment, a silent harbinger of the consequences she knew were coming. She felt a rift open between her parents and herself, deep and wide as a chasm.

Anastasia wanted to curl up in a ball of shame under her bed—disappear down a deep hole. Yet she had to know what was going on, what was happening to Paulo. Would he be all right? He had to be all right, she told herself. She sat on the floor against the wall in the corridor outside Paulo's room, her knees to her chest, invisible as her family tended to Paulo. Her Grandmother Lizabeth and Aunties Beatrice and Kadija had come over, a nurse, a doctor, and an herbalist respectively. They monitored Paulo's worsening condition, crushed herbs into powders, and made salves and potions for his wound. They hung an IV next to the bed and stuck a needle into his arm. Anastasia listened as they told her mother that they could delay the change, but no one yet knew how to stop it all together, much less reverse it.

There was no cure.

Her mother wept. Her father wept. Anastasia wept. Esmeralda stood guard outside the door. After seeing what the gardener's apprentice had done outside, Anastasia felt miserable but at least safe sitting next to her. Peter's training was indeed wondrous, and Anastasia looked on Esmeralda in a new light. Esmeralda, for her part, had always been tall for her age, taller than Anastasia, with golden skin, dark braids, and—although they were unseeing—gemstone-green eyes. Anastasia had once remarked to her mother how beautiful Esmeralda was and admitted her sorrow that Esmeralda could not see it.

"There is more important beauty than that which is skin deep and superficial," her mother had said. "And Esmeralda, being blind, knows that. It is a valuable lesson to know so young."

Anastasia's mother was often full of such insights, but right now she was only weeping and inconsolable. She would not leave Paulo's side. Anastasia knew better than to try to comfort her or even seek forgiveness. Anastasia was the root of the tragedy. She would only make things worse by showing her face to her mother. It didn't matter how remorseful she was.

Anastasia's father did emerge from the room, stopping outside the door to look down at her, but his words still would not come. His hurt, anger, and worry were all too great. She wished he would yell and at least begin the process of punishment. It would hurt, but it would at least be movement towards a place where everything would eventually be okay.

But maybe that place didn't exist anymore.

"Daddy, I'm sorry."

But he was already receding down the hall, covering his face with his hands.

"Sia, I'm sorry," Esmeralda said, her eyes unfocused but her expression sympathetic. "I know you didn't mean—"

"I wish I were dead. I wish he had bit me!"

"Sia, don't say—"

But Anastasia didn't hear the rest of Esmeralda's words. Instead she ran into her room and slammed the door shut behind her.

Hours passed. Anastasia cried herself to sleep, woke up from nightmares, cried more, fell asleep, the cycle repeating throughout the night. She knew by the light in the windows and the chirping of birds that morning had come, but the regular sounds of the house were conspicuously missing. Aside from the shuffling of feet in and out of her brother's room and a few muted whispers, a dreadful silence had descended on their entire compound. The normal noises of cooking, washing, and the gate opening and closing were all absent. She never realized how accustomed she had become to the clamor of Paulo running his mouth to their mother or to Peter the gardener. Paulo always talked too much, at least that was what Anastasia had told him. Now she regretted all the times she had not listened to him, all the times she had ignored him and failed to treasure his voice.

Anastasia cried some more. There was no point in getting out of bed.

It must have been midmorning when there was a knock at her door, followed by a voice.

"Anastasia, it is Peter. May I come in?"

She had already not followed the rules set down by adults and that had cost her brother his life. Anastasia was not about to ignore a request from Peter, especially since he had saved her life.

She got up and opened the door.

Old Peter stood there in his gardening coveralls. They fit his lean frame well and were always pressed, even if a bit faded in parts and the edges of the pockets frayed. His beard was gray and plaited into thick locks; his wide-brimmed red hat held down the hair on his head, even though it looked ready to pop out in a soft, springy explosion. He kept his head held up, as if to best capture signs and signals with the senses he did use: sounds, smells, even shifts in the air on his face. There was always a line of focus on his forehead that gave him a proud and attentive look. Anastasia had known him all her life to be a good listener, and sometimes, Anastasia felt, Peter "saw" her better than anyone.

Peter's eyes had golden brown irises. Like Esmeralda's, they were unseeing, yet she knew well how effectively he perceived the space around him. For that reason, she knew there was no need to escort him into her room. He could find his way. Instead she returned to her bed and curled up in a ball between her pillows. Peter took a few soft steps forward before sitting down on the edge of her bed, his hands resting on his cane, his back straight.

"How is Paulo?" she asked.

"Still unconscious. Your grandmother and aunts have him . . . comfortable."

"But the change?"

Peter frowned, his eyebrows gathered in. "To our knowledge it is irreversible."

She squeezed her eyes shut as tears began to flow again. "Peter, I'm so sorry. Thank you for saving me, but I wish, I wish it had been me."

"Shhhh, don't say that."

"But it's true Motinda," she said, using the name she had called him growing up. "This is the worst thing that could have happened. The worst thing I could have done."

Peter inclined his head downward and replied in a soft, gravelly voice, "You are right, Anastasia. It might be."

She would have cried again if she had not felt such a wave of humiliation at his words and a flare of anger that followed—one she directed at Peter, but she knew it was really at herself. "Did you come here to shame me?"

"No, I did not my little Starflower," he said reaching out for her, laying his hand flat on the bed between them. "I know your shame is already great. Your pain is punishment enough. I'm not here to add to it. That would serve little purpose."

She sniffed. "Then why did you come?"

"To urge you to have hope."

"Hope? How can I have hope when this is the worst thing—"

"Because this *is* the worst thing, and it is sometimes the worst thing that gives us opportunity."

Peter was speaking into the empty space in front of him, but she noticed how he inclined his head towards her, his ear picking up the way she shifted. She said nothing. She didn't understand, but he knew that he had captured her attention. "Let me tell you a story, Sia, like when you were little. Would that be all right?"

"Yeah . . ."

"Well, it is about a young boy who wanted to be a painter, a little brother like Paulo, by turns sweet, inquisitive, and maybe a little annoying, as little brothers can be." This he said with a knowing tilt of his head. "This boy had a big sister too, named Tamaret. He adored her and she had so many friends. He was always asking to tag along, which was a great source of irritation for her."

"I can understand that."

Peter opened his hands, relaxing his grip on his cane for a moment. "One time, this boy was sick with malaria, and while their parents were busy working—they were not a rich family and struggled to keep food on the table and to meet the costs of school books and uniforms—Tamaret was tasked with caring for her brother. Well, she resented being stuck at home when she wanted to go out with her many friends, but it was her job to give her brother his medicine every two hours. So in order to buy herself enough time to sneak out and meet up with her friends, she gave her brother double his normal dose of medicine so she could go out for *four* hours while he slept. He would be fine, and she would see her friends and be back before their parents returned. It was the perfect compromise. And her plan worked . . . or at least she thought it had. Tamaret went out and returned to find her brother sleeping. It was only when he woke that she realized her catastrophic mistake. She had ignored the warning label on the bottle. Too much medication at any one time could lead to irreversible side effects. In this case, it was blindness.

"She blinded her bother?"

"Yes."

"Wait, Motinda, was that boy . . . you?"

"He was."

Anastasia felt a hollow feeling inside her stomach and her head felt light. "I never realized . . ."

He nodded. "It is not a story I tell often, for people see much tragedy in it: a boy who wanted to be a painter, rendered blind, his dreams ruined, his sister so ashamed she ran away from home. We never knew what happened to Tamaret after that."

"Motinda, I'm so sorry."

Peter shrugged. "Many people have said the same when they hear this story. It is full of sorrows, and yet, can I tell you a secret?"

"Of course."

"The secret is, I've come to love the life I have been gifted." He paused a moment to let the words sink in. "Being blind has made me aware of other things I would have never known: the love and care of others who mentored me; the richness of the worlds of sound, smell, taste, and touch; the forgotten senses of temperature, movement, orientation in space; and I have still been able to expand my ability to create, maybe not with paint, but with life. Flowers, vines, trees, and bushes, even the sands of the rock gardens have become my canvasses. But those are not even the best gifts. The best gifts have been the children I have had the opportunity to mentor and teach to also live in a world without sight."

"Like Esmeralda."

"And many others."

"What she did with you in the garden, to the zombie boy . . . it was amazing."

Peter shrugged again, as if it was nothing, just as mundane as raking leaves, trimming a bush, or coaxing a vine to grow onto a trellis. For a moment Anastasia did feel some tranquility, as she pictured the serene spaces Peter had created over the years and the steady rotation of other blind children he would take under his wing for a few months at time before they grew independent and were able to set out into the world on their own. But the feelings were quickly overshadowed. These stories were not the same as her own. There would be no happy ending for Paulo. Anastasia began to cry again as she said as much.

"We don't know how this story will end," Peter said.

"You think he will be okay?"

Peter's pause spoke volumes before he said with a sigh, "I don't know. I think not."

"Then how can there be hope?" Anastasia asked, her voice cracking. Why had he told her the stupid story in the first place?

"Sometimes, while in the worst of times, we have to create our own hope and fight to claim our own purpose. I will not mislead you, Anastasia. It may take time and the way can be full of pain, but suffering ceases to be suffering when we can give a meaning to it.

This is a hard lesson to learn, and we need friends to remind us of it. But it is our only chance if we wish to persevere."

"I don't see—" Anastasia bit her tongue at her awkward word choice, but it didn't appear to insult Peter in the slightest.

"You will, Starflower, you will."

Anastasia woke from another shallow sleep, disturbed by nightmares and the tears sliding sideways across her face. Her pillow was dark and damp where they had been landing. She was still alone in her room, but her phone was vibrating. She didn't move to see who it was, instead letting it ring to voicemail.

The light had changed. It must have been afternoon. The lanes and streets of the neighborhood in a city under curfew were still eerie in their silence, although even in her sleep Anastasia had heard the gate rattle open, the coming and going of their vehicle, and the opening and shutting of doors, likely as her grandmother and aunts went back and forth, seeking medicines, pharmaceutical and traditional, to help her brother . . . delaying the inevitable.

If the Ministry of Health heard of her brother's condition or the zombie boy—where had they put him, she wondered—they would all be quarantined.

The phone buzzed, again. She let it go to voicemail again.

Then it buzzed for a third series of rings. Anastasia finally leaned over from her pillows and looked at the screen to see who wanted to speak with her so badly as to call three times. A picture of her cousin in the Kaliande Region appeared on the screen, her face dark under a bright yellow head wrap, her face characterized by sharp eyes and striking cheekbones. Underneath the profile picture was her name, Njambi.

Anastasia didn't want to talk to anyone really, but she would talk to her cousin. She clicked on the phone and her cousin's face appeared, in real time, on the screen against the backdrop of her bedroom. Njambi's hair was braided in medium-sized cornrows, with a few shiny wood beads and cowrie shells worked into the ends. She was wearing a purple T-shirt that read in three lines:

## Shirts with a haiku,

## They're sort of overrated,

## I will not wear one.

"Hey, Njambi."

"Sia, I heard the news. I'm sorry."

"Thanks."

"How's Paulo?"

"I . . . I don't know. They are slowing the change, but it's irreversible. I haven't left my room."

"Why?"

"Because it's all my fault . . ."

Anastasia took a few moments to master her crying then proceeded to relate the story of just how her brother had come to be bitten. Njambi listened. She was attentive, her eyes sympathetic while she made soft noises of assent, sympathy, or both. Like Peter, Anastasia had always known her cousin to be a good listener.

"So you see, Njambi, it's all my fault. I just wish I were dead."

Njambi's next words, even her tone, surprised her. "Anastasia, I need you to listen to me. This is very important."

Anastasia wiped her nose. "Uh, okay."

"You need to do something. It's going to mean pulling yourself together, leaving your room, even leaving the house."

"My parents won't ever let me."

"They won't even notice."

Anastasia sucked in her breath. Njambi was probably right. "But why?"

"I don't know if it will help Paulo, but it might be the key to turning this zombie thing around."

Anastasia had been so wrapped up in herself, she had not even asked Njambi how she was, how her family was, whether or not they too were trapped. They lived out in Kaliande, in the countryside, where the outbreak had begun after all.

"Njambi, I'm sorry, I didn't even ask. How are you, your family? Have you all been under attack? Are you surrounded, under curfew too?"

"We were. The zombies started out here, but they all headed away, to the capital."

Anastasia swallowed, imaging that if that were the case, millions of zombies would have been closing in on them, a sea of the undead, shamblers and runners surrounding the city in such numbers that supplies would eventually not get through.

"But why?

"I don't know, but I have some . . . friends who told me—"

"Which friends?" Anastasia asked. Her cousin had some notoriety in her family and in her village for having survived an ordeal of many days hiking into the wilderness and up the unforgiving slopes of Mount Kaliande to retrieve water from a spring that allegedly had healed her father, Anastasia's uncle, Murito. Some had even said that Njambi had returned in the talons of a giant mountain bird. Njambi did not talk about the experience much, and Anastasia knew how village people could exaggerate stories, but still, everyone regarded Njambi as wise, even her older sisters, who were all successful in their own right as businesswomen and entertainers. Anastasia had learned never to question Njambi. People in their family speculated that Njambi could even talk to spirits, but this was something else Anastasia's cousin was circumspect about.

"Uh, well, they are some friends I met once . . . but I still see them in dreams," Njambi said, her eyes darting off to the corner of her room.

"Njambi, you really are a seer then!"

"Shhhh, I don't know what to call myself. I just know from them that there is a woman—she's sort of a renowned philosopher-scientist from the Southern Region. She's a genius, and she's farther along in figuring out this plague than anyone else. But she is going to need your help."

"Mine? What could I do? How does she know me?"

"She doesn't . . . yet. You will have to explain to her. But I think she will get it. The institute she founded is located in your part of the city."

"Okay, okay, so what's the address? What is her name?" Anastasia asked.

"Do you have a pen and paper?"

Anastasia went to her desk, pushed aside her school books, and uncapped a pen. "Ready."

Njambi took a breath. "Her name is Dr. Latia Solei, MDiv, MD, PhD."

Anastasia wrote the name down and all the credentials too. If Njambi was mentioning them, they must be important.

"Wow, with all those letters after her name, she's got to know something."

"I hope so."

Njambi had been right. With everything going on at Anastasia's home with Paulo and his worsening condition, it was more than easy for her to move about the house, unnoticed, gathering a few things in preparation for sneaking out.

Njambi had given Anastasia the address for Dr. Solei's office at the Saitoti Research Institute. No taxis or buses were running, but Anastasia estimated she could walk there in thirty-five minutes or so. It was what might be waiting for her outside the safety of her family's compound that had her worried. She knew she would need her phone, as well as a backpack with snacks, water, rope, and even a first-aid kit, although she hoped she wouldn't need it. Otherwise, Anastasia kept the packing light—in case she had to run for her life.

She knew the reality of the dire situation zombies presented. She knew she would need to carry something to defend herself with. She stole a machete from the garden shed that was used for trimming grass and hedges. It was what her avatar would have done in the Killing Zombies—Africa Edition videogame. But in real-life, where zombies were real people, like her brother, she was not sure if she would ever be able to actually swing it . . . to hurt one.

But she took it anyway.

It was not difficult to slip out the door in the gate. Anastasia eased it open slowly so that the hinges did not squeak. The trickiest bit was closing it behind her and making sure the lock did not make too much noise clicking into place. With the zombie boy intruder and the threat of officials coming to quarantine their house, everyone would be listening for the slightest noise at the gate—especially with

Peter and Esmeralda as vigilant as they were. In the end, Anastasia knew some noise could not be helped and leaving the gate unlocked was unacceptable, as it would have put her family and friends at further risk. So she pulled it shut and simply ran, making sure that if anyone did come to look, she would be long gone by the time they reached the gate to peek out.

She finally stopped running after rounding two corners and ducking down a footpath between roads where local sellers had set up booths and stalls. They were all closed, as if it were a national holiday. Usually the footpath here was busy with pedestrian traffic: shoppers, hawkers, hagglers, and people sitting under umbrellas pitched over plastic tables and chairs while they drank soft drinks or tea.

But today there was not a single person. The footpath was empty but for a few candy wrappers rustling past in an anemic breeze and a half dozen used scratch cards for mobile phone airtime sunk into the mud. Above, the cloudy afternoon sky was a sickly shade of yellow, as if a sandstorm had swept over the city. It reminded Anastasia of pictures she had seen of the months the Harmattan would blow down from the Sahara in West Africa.

She wasn't sure why, but Anastasia kept running down the length of the lane. Maybe it was because she was still close to home and people here might recognize her. She pictured some of the booth owners hiding inside, looking out as she passed. When the lane ended at the T-junction of roads, which were also empty, she took the road leading west to the main highway.

The main road had wide margins on either side, with dirt footpaths packed down from the passage of thousands of feet every day. Tall jacaranda and Malindi flame trees grew in rows on both sides of the highway, providing shade on sunnier days. In normal times, people would be walking to the bus stops. Sellers would be roasting chicken, pork, and maize, or frying potatoes. Women would have been selling bananas, mangoes, or oranges to commuters who would toss the rinds to the ground. Men would be hawking mobile phone chargers and cases to people at bus stops.

But again, today things were desolate. Anastasia moved within the shelter of the trees, ducking from the cover of one trunk to the next. Here on the main road, she did see a car—an SUV with tinted windows—driving well over the speed limit as the driver and passengers rushed from one destination to the next, limiting their time outside in the wide open.

*Anyone would be crazy not to rush, I guess. Even crazier to be out on foot,* she thought.

The main road led right to the city center. Anastasia found herself hiding behind bushes and trashcans when other cars passed. Two Ministry of Health trucks went by in a convoy with police cars, as well as two more private cars. They all turned down the road leading to one of the only hypermarkets that remained open. It had high walls around the parking lot, so it had been able to keep its customers safe. It was the open-air markets that had been closed since early in the plague, since they had no walls themselves. But with the plague continuing, the zombie numbers growing, Anastasia wondered again how many more supply trucks would be able to enter the city to resupply even the hypermarkets.

When she reached the heart of downtown, Anastasia continued to jog, the backpack bouncing on her back, the machete growing heavy in her arm. No messages, no missed calls on her phone. No one had noticed she was missing. She spied a few people on foot. A tight bunch of men with sticks and machetes: a community-watch, patrolling for zombies. She hid behind some bushes until they had passed, as they would likely have sent her home if they had caught her. To her astonishment, she saw one man in running shorts, a headband, and earbuds jogging down the street. He had nothing in his hands to defend himself! He *did* have a nylon belt wrapped around his waist with little bottles of colored athletic drinks. He was white—of course—which made perfect sense to Anastasia. Foreigners often fell into two categories: those who walked about terrified of Africa, with bottles of bug spray, sunblock, and mace, and those who felt invulnerable and acted like they had no sense whatsoever. This man was clearly the latter. As he neared, she could hear the music blaring in his headphones. For him, she felt obliged to give up her hiding place and step out onto the sidewalk to warn him of the danger he was in, but he swerved around her, shouting, as if to hear himself over his music, "Sorry, me don't have any change to give you, little girl."

He padded away on his expensive running shoes. Anastasia rolled her eyes. *"Me don't have."* At least he was headed in the direction of the community patrol. Perhaps they would see him and talk some sense into him.

*White people.*

The neighborhood where Dr. Solei's research institute was located was a residential one and not hard to find. Anastasia felt some foreboding as she walked down the road into it, for all the homes had high walls around them and there were few lanes running between them. There would be few places to hide if she saw a community patrol . . . or worse.

But she had little choice, so she pushed onward, tracking her progress on a map she had copied out on notebook paper and double-checking the directions she had copied next to it. She wanted to save her phone's battery, and so she was not using GPS. The roads were easy to navigate, and she turned a few more corners, her confidence growing.

Until she realized she had a much more serious problem.

Anastasia had turned the last corner before the street the institute would be on, but right down the road, in the middle of her path, were two hunched and gruesome figures.

Zombies.

The closer of the two she could smell on the breeze. This was at least "good" news, since it meant that Anastasia was downwind. But there was nothing good about the odor. It was the stench of the grave, of a body rotting in a gutter, festering in the sun. This zombie was a shambler. It had been an old woman, who had likely died after a long life. Her funeral dress was moldy and ruined from ground water and decay. Her body was falling apart in grotesque ways: she was missing an eye, and the flesh around her legs was gone, so she walked on bones wrapped in loose stockings with a Swiss cheese pattern of holes in them. Entire chunks of her face were gone, revealing her jaw and teeth and a gray tongue lolling between them. Anastasia tried hard not to gag and hid herself around the corner of the nearest wall.

It was the farther zombie, she knew, that posed the greater threat. This one was only recently deceased and looked to have escaped the hospital morgue, for he was dressed in a hospital gown. A toe tag flipped along the ground as he moved along the gutter, sniffing for anything to eat. His body had yet to decay, and she knew he would be able to run after her if he caught her scent. But if her estimations were correct, the zombies were right between her and Dr. Solei's compound.

She would never get past them.

Anastasia crept backwards, the way she had come and unfolded her map. The neighborhood was set up with some semblance of blocks, and she realized she could go the long way around, sneaking behind the zombies, since they were moving towards where she was hiding now and away from the address she had for Dr. Solei. She refolded the notebook map, just as something screamed behind her.

She turned to see the terrible face of the old woman zombie, with its yawning, ruined mouth. The thing had rounded the corner, spotted her, and started towards her. Anastasia knew the other would not be far behind. She began to sprint away.

She worked out the turn she had to take in her head. Halfway down the next street though, she looked over her shoulder to see that indeed, the other zombie, his hospital gown flapping about him, was coming after her, eyes wide, mouth black and red with gore. She pushed herself to run faster, her lungs burning, the beats of her heart punching up into her throat. Her skin broke out in a cold sweat. She raced around the next corner, knowing she was taking a risk by not checking for more zombies first, but she couldn't afford to slow down. She was lucky; the street was clear. She could see the turn for Dr. Solei's road, but she could also hear the feet of the zombie slapping on the pavement as he turned the corner after her.

Anastasia had the machete, but she was more certain than ever that she didn't want to use it. There had to be another way. As she raced along the walls of compounds and locked gates, she looked up and thought of one.

Many of the compounds had trees with limbs that reached over their walls. She slipped an arm out of her backpack strap, pulling it in front of her, unzipped it, and yanked out her length of rope. The zombie was closing, his legs longer than Anastasia's, but she had picked out the tree limb she needed. She came to an abrupt stop, tossed the end of the rope over, and secured the most basic of knots with the end that fell down. She made the quick and difficult decision to drop the machete before she started to climb. It just would have gotten in her way.

*I hope I don't come to regret that.*

She used her legs and feet to supplement the strength of her arms, just as she had learned to do in gym class. The runner's breathing and groaning grew louder and closer behind her. The tree branch shook as she pulled herself up, the leaves rustling and a few grape sized yellow fruits—kumquats—dropping around her. She pushed and pulled up a bit further, the top of the wall coming into view. She could just see over it into the compound.

The zombie was just below her, hissing and clawing at the wall, too much of his pre-frontal cortex gone for him to understand how to use the rope himself. Anastasia got her hands on the tree limb, swung her legs up, and shimmied along its length until she could balance on the wall.

Her pursuer cried out in frustration, a piercing voice that warbled between a high-pitched scream and a low growl, like a hungry dog. She was, thankfully, out of his reach, as unreachable as the machete was to her, left useless on the ground next to the zombie's feet. The old lady zombie came shuffling around the corner too, prompting Anastasia to pull the rope back up, out of their reach.

*Just in case.*

She turned to take in the compound and felt a rush of gratitude. After a series of disasters, at least one lucky break had come her way: this was the very compound she wanted. She double checked the address above the door of the main building, though the sign over the door, "The Saitoti Research Institute," was enough to tell her she was in the right place. The grounds were well kept with orange and avocado trees, as well as potted frangipani set at even intervals along a brick path. But there were signs that gardeners had not visited in some time. The grass was high, and the walkway was dotted with the fallen petals of the frangipani blooms. Dozens upon dozens of kumquats were scattered, uncollected on the ground.

Anastasia made her way to the trunk and slid down it into the yard. The main house was a converted colonial estate, the original windows replaced by sleek, energy-efficient glass without sectioned panes. The roof was lined with solar panels, satellite dishes, and antennae. Crowded in the spaces between were weather instruments such as wind and rain gauges, lightning rods, and even barometers. She walked between the frangipani pots and stepped to the ebony door. It was carved with intricate Swahili reliefs common on the coast. To the left of the door waited a touch panel. An invisible electronic eye detected her and chimed, the screen flickering on to display a keypad and a field for a security code.

"Uh, hello?" Anastasia said.

After a few moments, the screen cleared and a voice came out from a speaker overhead. It was a female voice, confident, if a bit distracted. "Who are you? How did you get past the gate?"

"I am Anastasia Ailbe. I . . . I climbed over. I was running from zombies, but I was looking for the Saitoti Research Institute. I am looking for Dr. Solei. I know it sounds strange, but my cousin, she told me I should try to find Dr. Solei. See, my brother was bit by a zombie because I wasn't watching him, and my cousin, she, well, she . . . people say she can talk to spirits, and I think they told her that I should come here and that somehow Dr. Solei is the key to finding a way to fix the outbreak."

Anastasia knew she was rambling. She had not really prepared her story, and the adrenaline rush of the chase was still in her, making her speak at a breathless pace. She surely sounded like a foolish girl—maybe a bit crazy—but these were crazy times, and perhaps the unprepared nature of her story would lend her some believability. Anastasia paused, taking out a handkerchief and wiping her face and neck. Just as she stuffed it into her pocket again, the door opened.

The woman on the other side was older than she but still young. She looked like a graduate student, her hair in a gray wrap and wearing a white lab coat and a stylish pair of white-framed glasses that were a striking contrast to her dark complexion. The young woman took in Anastasia, her eyes looking up and down the length of her body, studying her sweaty, disheveled appearance, her full backpack, and her still heaving chest. The woman's eyes glanced out at the yard as if to confirm Anastasia was unaccompanied. She lifted herself onto the balls of her feet as she looked out, her movements smooth and poised, as if she were a professional dancer or had grown up balanced on the upper branches of a tree. It lent her an almost royal air.

"You came alone?" she asked.

"Yes."

"Please come in. I'm Dr. Latia Solei."

The interior of the building bore all the signs of having been converted and upgraded to a state-of-the-art scientific laboratory, but just what branch of science Anastasia was not sure. They passed through a room full of two-, four-, and six-legged machines that was clearly a robotics lab. Across the way was a chemistry laboratory with the standard glassware of graduated cylinders, beakers, and flasks. Gas extraction and sublimation apparatuses sat beneath dust covers. Against the walls were incubators, a fume hood, and an autoclave. The entire room hummed with the noise of a refrigeration unit in the corner.

A third room's ceiling extended upwards three stories to allow space for the enormous bulk of an astronomy telescope. It ended just short of the domed aperture in the roof—presently closed. Anastasia's head was on a swivel as she followed Dr. Solei up the staircase, the original polished wood steps and banister still intact. On the second floor they turned down a long corridor, passing by spaces that looked like student lounges with kitchenettes, white boards, and signs on the walls displaying the keys to the secured wireless network. Even though the building was designed to accommodate many teams of researchers, as far as Anastasia could see, Dr. Solei was all alone.

The doctor led her next into a series of rooms at the south end of the building. Here Anastasia's assumption that this was only a scientific institute fell apart completely, as they walked through rooms now lined with bookcases of old books, scroll fragments displayed in glass cases, as well as drawer after drawer of archeological artifacts. The next room was even more unexpected, as it was full of religious artifacts from around the world: talismans, statues, masks, and elaborately decorated headdresses. It was disorienting, like running through a museum without reading any of the signs: artifacts from historical and geological epochs, relics of dozens and dozens of cultures and belief systems, going by in a blur.

They went through a final corridor, where a row of windows facing the front of the house let light fall on a wall filled with plaques and paintings. Anastasia noticed a saying from Albert Einstein that read, "If you want your children to be intelligent, read them fairy tales." Another beside it read, "Uncertainty is the starting point of story; possibility, the end," but she didn't recognize the name, Jangwa, to whom it was attributed. Nor did she recognize the name, Father Richard Rohr, to whom the next saying was ascribed: "The problem is no longer to believe in God, it is to believe in humanity." She was equally unfamiliar with the name Peter Berger and the injunction next to his name: "See the general in the particular and the strange in the familiar."

The last bit of the wall had stylized African prints of a woman, perhaps even a goddess, in a swirl of burgundy robes, bedecked with sapphire earrings and necklace. She had piercing eyes and was walking on the steaming waters of a pool within a cave of ice. Across from the painting was a red and black wooden mask. It was hideous, with a screeching mouth, jagged fangs, and eyes of bottomless darkness. Anastasia felt a chill as she walked past it.

They finally stopped in a room that appeared to be Dr. Solei's study. Books from the sciences—physics, medicine, biology—were shelved next to texts on religion, folktales, and myths—many with cracked and peeling spines. Dr. Solei's desk, however, was state-of-the-art, with a new laptop docked and feeding into three display screens and three keyboards: one in Arabic, one with the Roman alphabet, and a third with Mandarin characters.

"Sit down, please. Let me make us some chai," Dr. Solei said.

Anastasia waited, studying the frames hung on the wall to her left. The degrees were less interesting than the photographs. She got up from her seat to take a closer look. The pictures had been taken in a village, perhaps Dr. Solei's home? The buildings in the background were rustic, made of clay with either thatch or tile roofs. The most prominent one was a red school house. A sign over its door read "Mti wa Anga Academy: Where the young can reach for new heights." Dr. Solei and a handsome young man in an apricot-colored dashiki stood side-by-side, cutting a ribbon before the school. The next picture had Dr. Solei and the same young man again, cutting a second ribbon, this time with some other members of the village in front of an even larger building with the name "Cirrus Secondary." The third had an even larger crowd gathered around Dr. Solei and the young man, again, as they cut a third ribbon before the doors of "Ndoto Hutimizwa University." The bystanders changed, as did Dr.

Solei's hairstyles, but she and the young man were constant, as was the look of genuine enthusiasm, even affection that the man with the preference for apricot dashikis wore as he looked at Dr. Solei in each picture.

Dr. Solei returned with a tea tray. Anastasia turned and rushed back to her seat, feeling as if she had been caught snooping. Dr. Solei did not seem to mind. She sat down, not behind her desk but in the other chair alongside so that she could sit next to Anastasia.

"You must be brave, stupid, or desperate, to come out here alone. They say the perimeter is being breached everywhere," she said, sipping her chai.

"Possibly all three?"

"That goes for all of us these days, doesn't it?"

"Yes." Anastasia had launched into her story, without restraint, earlier. That had gotten her in the door, but she had no idea who this woman was, aside from the fact that she was very learned. She didn't want to be rude and ask too many personal questions too soon, so Anastasia started with, "What is this place?"

"The Saitoti Research Institute. It's named after my father. He was chief of my village when I was growing up."

"Is that where the pictures are from?"

"Yes," Dr. Solei said, blowing on her chai to cool it. "Those were from the inauguration of different schools. They were the dream of my . . . friend."

Anastasia noted the slightest of pauses before the word "friend." Dr. Solei, who had shown no timidity to meet her gaze up to now, looked away. She stared for a long, wordless moment at the pictures. Anastasia wondered if Dr. Solei missed her home or maybe her "friend." She sensed there was more story there, but it wasn't her business. She needed this woman to help her, and Anastasia had appeared uninvited on her doorstep. She was not about to be nosy or presumptuous. Instead she nodded to the diplomas on the wall, "My cousin told me you had lots of degrees, but I never guessed so many. How do you find the time?"

Dr. Solei sipped her chai again. "Why sleep when you can read?"

Anastasia realized her parents probably would have wished she were as excited about studying.

"This cousin of yours, she had a dream that led you here? Tell me more."

Anastasia told Dr. Solei her story in greater detail, including the family legends about Njambi—her mysterious journey to Mount Kaliande—as she thought it might explain why Anastasia had listened to Njambi in the first place and risked her life on the streets on the mere hint of a dream.

Dr. Solei listened without judgment. If anything, she appeared interested, making curious "umhmms" and even saying "interesting" at times. When Anastasia finished relating what had happened with her brother the day before, her chai had gone cold. Dr. Solei had finished hers and replaced it on her lap with a notebook where she jotted down a few thoughts before she put the pen between her teeth and furrowed her brow.

Anastasia waited, swallowing. When Dr. Solei said nothing, the long silence becoming uncomfortable, Anastasia asked, "Do you have any idea why Njambi would send me to you, Dr. Solei?"

"Please, call me Latia."

"Okay, uh, Latia. So what do you think this is all about?"

Dr. Solei—Latia—answered with a question. "Do you believe in ghosts, Anastasia?"

Her mother, whenever Anastasia had been scared at night, had always told her there were no such things as ghosts. But in church they talked about souls and spirits. Jesus had cast out demons, and the priest often invoked the Holy Ghost. If all those things were so, maybe ghosts *were* real? Anastasia was not sure whether to believe her mother or the church ladies and priests.

"Well, recently we've seen that zombies are a thing, so maybe anything is possible. I don't know."

"'Admitting ignorance prepares the soil for the seed of wisdom,' or so the saying goes," Latia said. Standing, she walked over to the doorway they had first entered the office through and waved at Anastasia to follow. They retraced their steps through the house while Latia spoke. "I think this all has to do with zombies, ghosts, and *story.*"

"Okay . . ." Anastasia said, following behind Latia, if not following what she said. But Latia continued as they passed, again, through the artifact room, into the hall, and back towards the stairs.

"We all have bodies, Anastasia. Science tells us this. We have souls too. We know this from tradition, folktales, and theology. But it's when our souls become separated from our bodies that we can get into trouble. Normally the separation is easy. Bodies are left behind to sleep in the earth and become one with the next cycle of life, and the soul becomes spirit, and the spirit goes on to the afterlife . . . whatever that looks like."

Anastasia followed Latia down the staircase. "You mean Heaven?"

"It could be Heaven. It could be like Tian, Valhalla, Jannah, Svarga Loka, or the Summerland. Maybe you are reincarnated, maybe you join the ancestors. If there is one thing we have learned from Quantum Field Theory, it's that—in some sense—all possibilities exist simultaneously. Our illusion of absolute certainty, of binaries, this notion that reality is one thing that we observe but not the other, is an emergent phenomenon of our existence on a plane of reality governed by classical notions of gravity and relativity. At the quantum level, it's just the opposite."

"I'm so confused," Anastasia said as they reached the bottom of the steps, Latia turning and leading them into the chemistry lab. She went to the refrigeration unit and placed her palm on a security reader. A computerized female voice recognized her with a "Welcome back, Dr. Solei," as she opened the sealed door. Latia took a steel canister out of a case locked inside the fridge. Canister in hand, Dr. Solei led the way back upstairs. Anastasia scrambled to follow.

"Don't worry about the Many Worlds hypothesis just now. What you need to know is that if our spirits get lost, that is when they become ghosts. When you are a ghost, it means you have forgotten your most important truths, your notions of who you are; and if you are a ghost, your body becomes restless."

"So when you are a ghost, what is left behind becomes a zombie," Anastasia said, running up the stairs alongside Latia.

"Exactly."

"So we just need to reunite the ghosts with their bodies and the zombie problem is solved?"

"You're getting there, but it's a little more complicated," Latia said, leading them back to her office. "See the ghosts have lost something, forgotten it really."

"You said they forgot their truths, who they are."

"Right, they have forgotten their *stories.* Forget leptons, quarks, and bosons. The most fundamental element of the spirit realm is not physical, but *metaphysical.* It is the story, our narrative, with a beginning, middle, and end—resolution and identity being the emergent phenomenon from those pieces, just like atoms, molecules, and elements are emergent in the material world. And they, in turn, come together to make everything from teacups to particle accelerators."

Anastasia was pretty certain she was lost again.

They made their way through the series of rooms and hallways back to Latia's office where she sat down in her seat across from her desk again. Anastasia took her place next to her. This time

Latia's stare was intense and penetrating. "And if you don't know your story, Anastasia, you don't know the most important truths in the universe."

"The truth," Anastasia repeated. She thought of the church ladies and priests telling her how Jesus was "The Way, the Truth, the Light," or her Muslim friends explaining to her that the Quran was "Truth," even courtroom dramas on television where witnesses swore to "tell the truth and nothing but the truth." But what truth, little t or big T, was Latia talking about? Anastasia had no clue. Latia read her confusion.

"It's a conclusion I only came to realize after studies across many subjects. I first saw it in the scientific world. In molecular biology it is evident in the cycle of life: birth, life, death, then rebirth, regeneration, then life, death and so on. In general biology it's obvious in the process of evolution. In particle physics it's in the laws of thermodynamics. I saw it at the grandest of scales in astrophysics, in the violent supernovae deaths of stars and how that spreads the material for life throughout the universe. Anastasia, do you realize that every atom in your body, every element from the hydrogen and oxygen in your blood to the iron, potassium, calcium—all those minerals and micronutrients—they all were fused in the heart of dying stars moments before they exploded?"

Anastasia was not sure how to respond or if she was even tracking along with all that Latia was saying, but Dr. Solei had the degrees, ran a research institute, and Njambi had sent Anastasia to her, so she was inclined to trust her.

"Uh no, I had not realized that. . ."

Latia continued, apparently not discouraged by Anastasia's ignorance. "After that, I turned to the qualitative disciplines. I saw it everywhere: ethics, metaphysics, and epistemology. The same pattern emerges in theology and history, not to mention literature and poetry. I saw fragments of the same truth everywhere I looked. After all this time, I can boil it down to this: it all comes down to the power of story, specifically the *redemptive story.*"

"Redemptive story," Anastasia repeated, thinking she was starting to understand. This sounded a bit like Sunday school class or a teaser for a drama on television.

"I'm not talking about Jesus," Latia said, as if sensing just what Anastasia had been assuming.

"Oh."

"Although Jesus is sort of the Christian version of this story," she added. "But that is just one lens, one possibility existing among the many."

"Okay," Anastasia said, twisting one of her braids.

Latia leaned forward, her eyes sympathetic, as if she knew she was overwhelming Anastasia's thirteen-year-old brain. "It's like this. The redemptive story is the notion that we *need* transformation stories. We need stories wherein the bad is redeemed by its ultimate good, by someone rising above their suffering. We need to see how others learn lessons from their travails, to become better people than before. It's the idea that what you lose, what you suffer can become a doorway to something better."

Anastasia was back in her room, listening to Peter Motinda. "I think . . . I think I actually know what you are trying to say."

"You do?"

"Yes, it's a bit like something my friend Peter Motinda told me earlier today."

"That is a notable coincidence. Perhaps not a coincidence at all."

"But Dr. Solei, what does that have to do with zombies and ghosts?"

"Well, this truth, this redemptive story, it's the underlying truth to our existence in the universe. But when the soul forgets it, it wanders as a ghost, and ghosts end up in dangerous places. I'm speculating a bit now, but my theory is that, for some reason, the dead of our country have become ghosts and they are getting lost. I think they are in Limbo."

"Limbo?"

"Yes, it's a sort of wasteland. And the longer they stay there, the more they forget. If they forget too much, they will never be able to return here or go forward to whatever vision of the afterlife they expect."

"But why are they forgetting?"

Latia frowned and shook her head. "That, I don't know. It could be black magic, but I'm still trying to figure it out. I had my team helping me, but I sent them home to check on their families. I couldn't justify keeping them here."

Anastasia rubbed her temples. She had a bit of a headache from all the information she was trying to process. If there were zombies and ghosts, she guessed she could accept there was such a thing as black magic too. "So what do we do?"

"Someone has to go into Limbo. Someone who can lead the ghosts back to the Path where they can remember their stories."

"The Path?"

"Think of it as the main highway of the afterlife. It branches in a lot of different directions, to different afterlives. One of those branches, a dead end one, is Limbo."

"I don't quite see the connection. Stories are not truth. They are made up."

Latia raised a finger. "That is not as clear cut as you think. There might be more fact in fiction than not. The best stories, the timeless ones, they are like pulling a single thread and as you pull that thread it grows thicker, turning into a string. You keep pulling, the next thing you know you are hauling in a rope, the rope becomes a cable, then the cable a chain, and it turns out the chain connects to the rest of the universe."

Supernovae, ghosts, heaven, death, strings, chains, the universe. Anastasia shook her head as if clearing it after a sneeze.

"I know it's a lot to take in," Latia said, leaning back now, her hands folded on her lap.

Anastasia tried to shrink the spinning world down to something manageable. She reminded herself why she had come in the first place, remembering the series of events: her failure, her brother's worsening condition. "I . . . I just want to help Paulo get better." She swallowed a lump in her throat. "What do I have to do to help?"

"Are you sure you want to help?"

Anastasia pictured her brother, his skin shading to blue-gray, the color in his bright brown eyes fading, the sad, drawn faces of her grandmother, her aunties, the tears on her parent's faces.

"Yes."

Latia got up and stepped over to her desk, where she had set the flask from the lab. She turned its top and it opened with a click and a hiss. The liquid she poured out of it into a graduated cylinder was a light purple. Anastasia thought she might have caught the scent it gave off from where she sat, but she had never encountered a liquid with such a strong scent of the sea breeze. It brought to mind vacations to the coast with her family when her grandparents were still living and all three generations of her family could interact.

Latia stirred the liquid in the beaker with a glass rod, looking over to Anastasia with a smile. "What do you smell?"

"It's like the sea, when my whole family would go to the beach . . . I was so happy then."

"I smell laundry."

"Laundry?"

"Clean laundry, that is," Latia smiled. "It's one of my earliest memories: looking up into the lines of linen just as my mother was hanging the wash out to dry in the sun. I was on her back. I could feel the vibration of her voice inside me while she sang. I was against her warm, breathing body, close enough to touch her face."

Latia stood, holding the beaker and taking a deep breath over it through her nose, her eyes closed. Anastasia was surprised to see a tear form at the corner of her eye.

"Do you miss your mother?"

"I do. She died when I was very young. And my father, he sent me away. I was raised by teachers and mentors. He said it was so I could be successful and educated, which is what happened. But I also know it was because . . . well even then I looked like my mother, and I think it broke my father's heart to be reminded of her."

"I'm sorry . . . but how can I smell one thing and you another?"

Latia wiped her eye, her scholar's face returning. "It's the nature of empyreum. It took my team and me years to determine the exact molecular composition of it from herbalists, shamans, medicine women. Then our chemists, physicians, and pharmacists had to reverse engineer it. We found it never smells the same to two people. Here, you will want to lie down."

Latia lifted the cylinder as if making a toast towards the window. They crossed the room to where a leather sofa, the kind you might find in a psychologist's office, was waiting. It was big for Anastasia, her feet barely reaching halfway down its length once she settled into its arm. Latia held the beaker out to her. "You have to drink this."

"I was afraid you would say that."

Latia offered a sympathetic smile. Something about her expression, the kindness and wisdom behind it, soothed Anastasia's nerves. She took the beaker.

"What does it taste like?" Anastasia asked, looking down into the empyreum. It was thick and opaque, with a surface that reflected light with an almost metallic quality.

"It's actually indescribable," Latia said, pulling over a cart full of medical monitoring equipment.

"What will happen after I drink it?"

The cart had a laptop, a CPU, as well as a display screen. A box with dials on it connected all the hardware. The box had an array of electrodes running out of it, each ending in a soft pad. Latia handled the equipment with the familiarity of a trained technician. She used some alcohol wipes to prep the skin around Anastasia's temples before sticking the pads there. A series of flat lines on the display screen began to dance in waves and troughs. Another pad went over her heart. Next Latia brought over a blood pressure cuff and took a reading.

"You'll fall asleep. It will be like dreaming," Latia explained, checking the readout of the machine and adjusting the pads on Anastasia. "As for Limbo, I'm not sure what it will look like, but you should find all the ghosts of the zombies there, including your brother. You'll have to speak to them and try to bring them back to the Path. My hypothesis is that once there, they should remember and go on to where they need to go. The runners should return to their bodies, and the shamblers to the afterlife. But don't stay too long, because you'll forget your own story."

"Okay, seems simple enough."

"Yes," Latia said, pausing, a shadow of worry moving across her face. "You are brave, Anastasia. I don't know what else you will see there, or who. But I can warn you that there is one terrible demon that is supposed to be able to come and go at will in Limbo."

"A demon?"

"He doesn't even have a true name. He . . . she . . . whatever, is the spirit of death, destruction, chaos. Some think of him as a trickster, Exu, Legba, Elegua. In some traditions he is a coyote, others a fox. In stories he appears as a raven, a spider, or a rabbit. Some say he's really benign like Prometheus, or malevolent like Satan, or something in-between like Kali."

"And if I see him?"

Latia pierced her with a glare. "Run."

Anastasia swallowed another painful lump in her throat. She looked into the empyreum. "All right, I guess it's best to just get this over with."

"Hold on, let me check your baseline."

Latia tapped a few keys on the laptop while Anastasia continued to stare into the mysterious substance. It looked to be still and moving at once. She was not sure if it reflected the light, let light shine through, or was actually glowing. All too soon, Latia said, "Ready."

Anastasia tipped the glass back, poured past her lips and swallowed. The empyreum had the consistency of warm honey. The taste as it bloomed in her mouth was something she could best describe as "purple and cerulean." It was warm as sunlight, but after she swallowed, the finish in her mouth and nose was cold, as cold as wind passing through the emptiness of space.

"You're right," she said to Latia, a little overwhelmed by the sense of harmony and discord at once. "It is indescribable."

"I know."

Anastasia stared up at the ceiling, but her eyes darted back to Latia. "I don't feel very sleepy."

"That is because there is one more ingredient," Latia said, turning the screen aside and pulling her chair close.

"What is it?"

"A story, of course," Latia said, her hands pressed together between her knees.

"Of course, a story . . . sure. But uh . . . which story?"

"That is the fun part. Any story, you get to choose."

"Like . . . a bedtime story? This doesn't seem too scientific," Anastasia said.

"Do zombies, ghosts, and magic potions seem *scientific*?"

"Well no, but you did hook me up to a heart monitor, and you are wearing a lab coat."

"Touché," Latia winked. "But we have to hold space for all these things, all these lenses. And like I said, the root of this predicament is one of story. The story, with its beginning middle, and end, is the smallest unit of truth. Your story, my story, your brother's story. There is a sort of magic to them, especially the variant of the bedtime story. Doesn't matter which, just as long as I send you off with one."

"You're the doctor," Anastasia said, trying to settle back into the cushions of the couch. Her eyes fell on the far wall and the series of pictures of Latia and her friend opening the schools.

"Who is that young man in the dashiki next to you in all the pictures? How did you two meet?"

"Oh," Latia turned to the pictures. With one hand she fumbled with the lapel over her breast, pressing it down, with the other she rolled a stray braid back behind her ear. *"That* is the story you want to hear?"

If Anastasia didn't know better, she would have said the poised, accomplished, and accredited scholar-doctor was flustered. Had Latia's complexion been lighter, she might have blushed.

"Is he your boyfriend?" Anastasia asked, surprising herself with her own brazenness.

"Oh, uh, Jamhuri, I mean Dr. Jamari, I . . . uh, he is an old, childhood friend."

"You all look happy together."

"Well, we founded some schools back in our village. . ."

"You all must work well together," Anastasia probed. She was usually not so insistent. She wondered if the empyreum was loosening her inhibitions, like when she was extremely tired or how adults became when drinking wine. Her head did feel a little light, as if she were sleepy. "Do you see him a lot still?"

"Uh, not enough," Latia said, turning back to the display, her pen in her teeth. "We're both so busy. He runs the school and me with the institute. . ."

"So how did you meet?" Anastasia was definitely feeling groggy, and she didn't want to fall asleep without hearing the story and cause things to go wrong.

"Well," Latia said, removing the pen from her teeth and pushing her glasses up off her face so they perched on the top of her head. Anastasia could see that without them, Latia was exceedingly beautiful. "Like I said, my mother had passed away and my father had sent me away to learn where no one would reach me, a tree of all places. . ."

Anastasia listened, her consciousness slowly drifting as the story unfolded, shifting seamlessly between folktale and fact. She followed the twists and turns as best she could, fading as she was. Latia painted a picture of a tree that reached so high into the heavens that it had a dusting of snow on its branches and a brash young man determined to reach the top by any means he could. Talking monkeys, angry hippos, flocks of flamingos, and prayers to the gods mingled in Anastasia's mind, like fleeting visions of a long-lost memory, before she dropped off into a deep sleep.

◄❂►

Before she opened her eyes, Anastasia heard a light *plink, plink, plink, plonk.* It was a soft sound, something like water dripping and splashing, but somehow different by the slightest degree. She listened a bit longer. She felt as if she were in bed, just waking up on a Saturday morning. There was no hurry to rise. *Plink, plink, plink, plonk. Plink, plink, plink, plink, plonk.* Sometimes the sound came in a series of four, sometimes five. The intervals diminished between each successive *plink.* At one point, when it came in a series of seven, she heard a girl's voice say, "Yes!" as if exclaiming to herself.

Realizing that she was no longer in Latia's office, Anastasia opened her eyes and sat up.

She rose from a pool of liquid. It was clear as distilled water; not cold, not hot, rather, it felt the same temperature as her skin, so that it almost felt like nothing at all. Anastasia didn't seem to be wet from it either. The only way she could even tell it was there was by how the light glimmered on its surface and how her own body beneath was distorted and wavered as it would if under water. She felt a resistance as she drew her fingers through it. The viscosity was somewhat less than water. As she tried to cup it in her hand, it evaporated, only leaving the faintest traces to trickle between her fingers and dimple the surface below.

*Plink, plink, plink, plink, plonk.*

Anastasia turned her head to the source of the noise. The spot she was in was actually a shallow pool off to the side in a whole stream of the mysterious liquid. On a bank jutting out into the wider body of the stream, standing amid silvery blades of grass, was a girl about Anastasia's own age, skipping stones. Anastasia immediately recognized her and gasped. Esmeralda turned at the sound. She was wearing her green skirt and orange body wrap with a sash and head wrap in a complementary shade of green. Her staff was on the ground next to her, the long grass blades folded beneath it. Her eyes shone, in turns, shades of gold, amber, and green.

And she was *looking* at Anastasia.

"Anastasia! Hi!"

"Esmeralda? You can see?"

Esmeralda shrugged. "Sure."

"But . . . how did you recognize me?"

"It's the spirit world, who knows how anything works."

"But, what are you doing here?"

Esmeralda shrugged again, as if meeting Anastasia here was the most ordinary of things. She skipped another stone: *plink, plink, plink, plonk.* The sky was full of silvery clouds, the light diffuse. Anastasia wasn't sure where it was coming from.

"When I dream, I come here," Esmeralda said.

"And you can *see* here," Anastasia asked, looking into those disconcerting eyes of shifting hues.

"Oh yeah, of course."

"Where are we?"

Esmeralda looked around at the clouds overhead, the river meandering past them as if the question had never really occurred to her. "I don't know. Where are any of us when we dream? Can I help you up?" she said, after skipping a final stone out across the river.

"Uh, sure."

As Esmeralda pulled Anastasia up to the bank, more details of the space materialized. A gravelly shore of perfectly smooth black stones was underfoot. Further pools stretched in both directions as banks on either side of them traced serpentine paths between liquid and land.

"What is this stuff?" Anastasia asked, scooping the liquid in her fingers only to watch it disappear again.

"It's aether," Esmeralda said. "Just like the clouds and the air here."

"Aether . . . How do you know?"

"I'm not sure," she said, looking up and down the length of the stream. "How does anyone know anything in a dream?"

Anastasia was detecting a theme.

"But I don't think I'm dreaming. I drank a potion at Dr. Solei's research institute. I'm supposed to try to bring Paulo back."

"Oh yeah, I'm remembering now," Esmeralda said, her eyes widening. "You went missing from the house. You snuck out, you cheeky girl, you. Your parents are worried."

"They are?"

"Oh yeah, they're wrecks. They realized you were missing this afternoon. I'd been up all night standing guard outside Paulo's room and Peter had just relieved me. I would have helped search for you, but Peter insisted I rest. So I went to my room and fell asleep. That's when I came here."

Anastasia felt a wave of guilt that she had caused her parents more anguish. But if it was necessary to save Paulo, she knew it had to be done.

"So, I'm in your dream?" Anastasia asked, looking around.

"Not exactly. Like I said, I come here *when* I dream, but it's not my dream, it's . . . a place."

"A place?"

"Sort of. I guess you wouldn't have been here before, as a seer."

"A seer?"

"A sighted person. When you see and take it for granted, you miss a great deal. Peter has helped me understand that one of the gifts of being blind is to see the spirit world and travel into it when my body is resting. We're in part of it now."

Anastasia felt a strange sort of shame and jealousy. Did everyone know more about the world than she? How could she have missed so much?

"The spirit world is huge," Esmeralda continued. "Much bigger than our own and full of things you'd never imagine and some things you might. It's where heavens and hells and all sorts of afterlives and before-lives reside."

"Then I think I'm in the right place. I am supposed to find Limbo."

"Huh, well that is interesting, because we're right there."

"This place? This stream?"

"Well, not exactly. This stream is the center of things. It's time and it flows in one direction. That flow is called the Path."

"Oh, I'm supposed to find that too."

"Makes sense. The Path is the center of things. You can travel up or down it or off to the worlds and times to either side. This bank here does really lead to Limbo. Maybe I'm here to lead you."

"Is that how things work here?"

Esmeralda shrugged once more. "As much as anything 'works' here. It's different."

"I'm gathering as much. Dr. Solei—Latia—she's a sort of scientist, doctor, medicine woman, and she said that zombies are a result of spirits forgetting their stories, leading them to become ghosts, and then they wander into Limbo and get stuck and need to be led out. If we lead them out, then the zombie problem will be fixed."

"Yeah? It's doesn't sound like a bad theory."

"Well, she called it a hypothesis. I guess I'm supposed to test it," Anastasia said, reaching for the terminology from her science classes and glad she could remember it. It kept her from feeling completely stupid, since it seemed like everyone else knew more than she did.

"Well then, let's go," Esmeralda said, bending to pick up her walking staff. Here it was transformed, longer than it was in real life, and sturdier. It was carved from yellow yew wood. Esmeralda started into the mists of aether, Anastasia following. As she did, something strange happened. The ground shifted. Anastasia's sense of up and down and the horizon shifted. She had to steady herself on her feet to keep from falling over. Esmeralda spun around, looked at her, and reached out to catch her—she would have to get used to Esmeralda being able to do that— Esmeralda held her arm in a firm, reassuring grip.

"Sorry, I forgot about that."

"What happened?"

"Things, perspectives shift here when you enter a different space," Esmeralda nodded backwards. Anastasia followed her gaze and experienced a second wave of disorientation and vertigo. The stream, or Path, had shifted as they had moved. Now, instead of flowing like a river, the stream moved upwards now, like smoke from an offering fire. Oriented so, Anastasia could sense how it had flowed up, out of the deep well of time, the past a land below them, the future ascendant.

"This is so strange," Anastasia said.

"This is just the beginning," Esmeralda said, helping to steady her. "Come on."

They walked for what felt like a few hours, but time was hard to measure in the spirit plane. There was no sense of fatigue and no bodily reminders, like hunger or thirst, that signaled a passage of time or the waxing or waning of energy. And on the one hand, it felt as if they had just arrived. But Anastasia knew they had been walking a while. It was much like the way time was compressed in a movie, jumping from one scene to the next, knowing an interval had passed, without clear memory of having experienced it.

As they walked, the "land" became somewhat more substantial. The ground was rocky and dusty, a bit like pictures Anastasia had seen of Mars, but the regolith here was dull brownish-gray, a sort of beige, lacking any distinct coloring at all. The landscape was featureless too, with no trees, shrubs, bushes, or any sign of growing things. And although the close curtains of aether had cleared, banks of it still hung just a few meters to all sides, so that their field of view was short. Even the sky pressed close, gray-white—a solid, opaque lid. When they came to a modest-sized ridge, Anastasia was exceedingly grateful for the small break in the monotony, even if it meant they would have to climb.

Anastasia had known they'd been walking and talking a long while, because in that time she had learned all about Esmeralda's life and how her family had struggled to cope with her blindness. Anastasia realized their world was one built disproportionately on sight and that it was hard to navigate for those with visual impairments or special needs.

"I don't even like either of those terms, 'impaired' or 'special needs.' I just call myself 'special,'" Esmeralda said.

Anastasia stopped herself short of saying "I see," instead choosing to say, "I understand."

Esmeralda shared how she had first met Peter, and how his training had transformed her life. She explained that she had learned to experience the world through other senses and discover things hidden to seers. As Anastasia listened, she regretted never having asked Esmeralda more about her life before, for the way she described her world of sounds, scents, textures, and tastes made Anastasia appreciate the world in a new way.

"It almost sounds as if you don't regret being blind," Anastasia offered as they began to climb.

"No, I don't. I'm used to it now. Peter helped me see how my 'disability' was actually a strength; my hurt, an invitation to learn gratitude and heal."

"Oh wow," Anastasia said, Esmeralda's words resonating with things Peter and even Latia had shared with her not long before. "So one of the 'benefits' is that when you dream you come here?"

"Apparently."

"And you've been to this place, Limbo, before?"

"Yes, but not a lot. It's not a safe place. Peter has warned me of it. If you stay too long, you forget the way back. It's kind of a sad place, too. The people you meet there have lost their memories. Nothing ever gets finished." Esmeralda paused for a moment before adding, "It's also dangerous because this is one of the realms where the unnamed one is known to stalk."

"The unnamed one," Anastasia said, something Latia had said resurfacing in her memory with a sinking sense of dread.

"Yeah, sounds cryptic, I know," Esmeralda said, in an apologetic tone. "But the 'unnamed one' is sort of his name."

"What is he?"

"A demon, a devil, a blight, a devourer of souls. I'm not sure exactly. I just know Peter tells me to go the other way, and fast, if I ever see him."

"Do you know what he looks like?"

"Never seen him, but I imagine him with a long red-and-black face, blue tongue, fangs—you know, nothing short of satanic."

Anastasia pictured the painting in Latia's office. At this point, the coincidence between that figure and the one Esmeralda "imagined" no longer surprised her. "Sounds about right. Latia told me if I saw something like that to run."

"Well, let's hope we get lucky. We're almost there—look."

They had reached the crest of the ridge. The expanse of land on the other side was no different than the wasteland they had already crossed, except on this side there was what looked like the ruins of a town. The buildings were stone and arranged in streets and lanes that met at right angles. But the buildings were oddly shaped and in various states of disrepair . . . or repair, as some looked to have incomplete frames of scaffolding around them. But not a single building was complete. The upper levels petered out, the scaffolding missing struts, footboards, or crossbars. The buildings themselves were capped with half-finished rooms missing walls, roofs, even floors. It reminded Anastasia of pictures she had seen of shelled out towns in Syria or Afghanistan.

"What is this place?"

"No one has gotten around to naming it. Sort of goes with the spirit of the place—no pun intended," Esmeralda said, her voice flat as she started down the hill.

As they reached the edges of the town, Anastasia saw her first people. They sat in doorways or courtyards or walked the streets, staring out with expressionless faces. She saw a handful of women and men, walking with baskets on their heads or backs full of rocks. They turned a corner, heading towards some place of construction.

"They must have just gotten here," Esmeralda said. "When people are new, they still want to *do* things."

The last one in the bunch was looking down at his feet so he didn't stumble and didn't see which corner the others had rounded. He looked about, his eyes passing right over Anastasia and Esmeralda. When he could not find his companions, indifference set in. He sat down, lost, given up, staring straight ahead like all the other people they had passed.

Farther down the street, Anastasia and Esmeralda came across a man who would walk a few feet in one direction before he would turn around, walk back a few steps in the opposite direction, then turn around again, repeating the process. It made her sad just to watch. Closer now, Anastasia could see that construction on many of the buildings had started numerous times with one type of stone, been abandoned, then started again with a different type. She noticed children's toys—trucks and cars made of wire like she would often see out in the villages—but these too were discarded and unfinished.

As they walked towards the center of town a few people followed them, not unwelcoming but not welcoming either. Esmeralda tapped her cane ahead of her, as if out of habit. She offered tentative "hellos" and waves. People mumbled back, their eyes darting back and forth, as if nervous. Anastasia offered a few greetings as well. Unsure what time of day it was, she dispensed with "good morning" or "good afternoon" and offered her own awkward, "hi." One man went as far as to raise his hand, but then dropped it, looking confused. It reminded her of people with autism who were unable to read social cues.

"It's like they have forgotten how to relate," she said.

"Some have, depending on how long they have been here," Esmeralda answered, her voice heavy with sympathy. "But they can sense we're different, that's why they are following."

Anastasia checked over her shoulder. Esmeralda was right. A crowd had grown behind them, with more people drifting out of alleyways and buildings to join. They were still aimless. They did not speak and showed only the merest hint of curiosity. But the numbers still grew. As they passed more lanes, roads, and intersections, Anastasia realized that the town was quite large, a city almost. Hundreds, even thousands of people lived among the half-finished buildings. The incomplete stories disappeared against the bland sky like fragments of broken dreams.

"How will we find Paulo?"

"He'll find us," Esmeralda said. "We just need to keep walking to the center of town."

They did, finally reaching a wide, open plaza that stretched the length of many blocks. In any normal town, this was where the market might be. Indeed, some people had begun to set up a few stalls, but without exception, none were finished; each lacked a wall, a roof, a corner beam, or sign, not to mention anything to sell.

Esmeralda and Anastasia wandered, a bit aimless themselves, from one corner of the plaza to another, Anastasia following Esmeralda's lead. Esmeralda continued to pass among the people, the colors of her clothes, even her skin more vibrant than anything in the sea of lost souls. Her eyes were deep and expressive, more expressive than Anastasia remembered in the material world.

The two of them came upon a group of boys and girls about Paulo's age. As Anastasia studied their faces she heard her own name.

"Anastasia?"

She turned. Amid a group of boys seated against a wall that was half gray and half white with whitewash, was Paulo. He looked the same as ever. Anastasia's insides leapt to see his familiar face among all the unfamiliar ones. And yet, he was changed. He shared the apathetic look of all the other ghosts, his expression barely registering his surprise as he looked upon his own sister. As Anastasia moved closer, she could see the striking contrast between Paulo's skin and her own. Like all the other ghosts, her brother's flesh was ashy and gray, as if it needed moisturizer or the dust of this parched land had settled on him, staking its claim to his soul.

"Paulo," she cried, taking his hands then pulling him close for a hug. He did not return it, his arms hanging limp at his sides.

"Anastasia, what are you . . ." he started to say, his words coming slowly before his voice trailed off.

"Paulo, Esmeralda and I are here to rescue you, to rescue everybody."

"Oh, hi, Esmeralda. It's nice . . ." Paulo said, as if noticing her for the first time. The fact that she could move without her cane and that her eyes were open and focused on the world around them made no impression on him.

"Paulo, are you all right?"

Her brother shrugged. "I guess. I don't really know. It's mostly boring. . ." He kicked a stone. Anastasia looked over to Esmeralda.

"This is what it's like for them here," she said.

"We were going to start a football game, but it sort of ran out of steam . . . people wandered away . . . we didn't finish making . . ."

Anastasia noticed Paulo looking over at a ball made from rags and twine, but no one had finished tying the knots together or gathering enough rags to make the ball the right size.

*Nothing finished. Not even a sentence.*

"Paulo, I'm sorry I let you down, but we're going to get you out of here. You and everyone else."

"Okay," he said, sitting back down among the other kids, who just stared out as if in a trance. The most engaged of them were drawing in the dirt.

"That means we're going *now,* Paulo," Anastasia said, her voice strained with a note of desperation.

"Go where, again? I'm sorry. I forgot what . . . what we were . . ." Paulo blinked his eyes and a crease formed across his brow for a few moments before he seemed to forget trying to remember all together.

"We'll just have to take charge," Esmeralda said. "Good news is that they are like sheep. They'll follow. We just need a shepherd."

Esmeralda struck the end of her staff against the nearest wall. It let out a series of cracks that echoed back from across the plaza many times over.

"Hear ye! Hear ye!" Esmeralda called out like a medieval town crier.

"'Hear ye, hear ye?'" Anastasia repeated. If things were not so dire, she would have burst out laughing.

"It was what I heard in a Shakespeare play once, or maybe it was Marlowe. I don't know. All those dead white dudes look the same to me."

Anastasia tried to pick her words carefully. "'*Look* the same' . . . ? But Esmeralda, you're . . . blind."

"I know, right?" Esmeralda laughed, then dropped her voice lower. "I wonder what *their* excuse is." She turned her face to the crowd, clearing her throat before she projected her next words, taking a different track this time "People of Earth! We are here to help you and return you to where you belong."

This time Anastasia did laugh, feeling a surge of affection for Esmeralda as she switched from Elizabethan English to 1950s camp.

*If we get out of this alive, I need to hang out with her more.*

The crowd murmured, more people joining from the side streets and alleyways, shuffling along, slower than Anastasia would have liked, but joining nonetheless. She kept Paulo next to her, his hand in hers.

"Where do we belong?" a middle-aged man asked.

"Not here," Esmeralda said. "You all are ghosts. Some of you still have living bodies, some of you have died, but this is not your final destination. You need to follow us. We will lead you out of this place, this Limbo. Then you can find the Path again and know where you belong.

A few more nods, a few shrugs. No one seemed to care too much either way, which was why Anastasia was glad when an old woman with thick gray locks said, "I think she's right. I have never felt like I was supposed to be here. I am supposed to be with my ancestors, and that is not any of you."

Another Indian man said, "And I am supposed to be reincarnated, to continue the cycle of samsara."

"If this is the afterlife, it is pretty boring," a thin old man said.

"I don't want to be dead. I don't think . . ." a teenage boy said, but could not complete his sentence.

"You might not be dead," Esmeralda encouraged them. "While you are here, some of your bodies are going around as zombies, wreaking havoc on the world. Come with us so we can put a stop to it."

Apathetic and forgetful as the ghosts were, they were responsive to whatever idea was placed in their heads. The trickle of a crowd grew into a stream and then a flood. Esmeralda cut a path through their numbers to the front to lead them back the way she and Anastasia had come. But another man cried out, "Wait, wait, aren't we here in this town for a reason? I can't . . ."

"He's right," another woman said, coming to a stop, the people around her stopping as well. "Remember, there is . . . oh, what was it?"

"That thing . . ." another person said.

"Oh yes," a few people added, while others clicked their tongues and sucked their teeth. Yet still others looked completely lost.

"What thing?"

"The monster. The one with the red and black face and the white things . . ." The teenage girl speaking curled her fingers in front of her face in the place of fangs.

"Teeth?" someone said.

"Fangs!" said another.

People snapped their fingers. "That's right."

Others were still lost. "What were we talking about? Why is everyone snapping?"

"The monster, it's tall as a tree!"

"As a mountain."

Anastasia felt a tremor in her body: the thing without a name.

"It will devour us."

"We can't leave."

The momentum was shifting. People began to sit back down and wander off, but Esmeralda rallied them.

"No, no, no. Anastasia and I have special powers. We can protect you against the unnamed one."

"The Devourer of Souls?" someone asked.

"Well, if you want to call him that. Maybe we could call him something less scary, like . . . I don't know . . . like Shorty McShortface."

"He's not short," someone in the crowd said.

"Okay, fine, call him Cecil Higgenbottoms, or Tinkles, or Bob, whatever you want, but we won't let him hurt you. Just follow me."

The mood shifted again. People were standing upright, gathering once more into groups. Esmeralda held up her staff. The end of it began to glow like a yellow flame in the dim light. The people resumed following. Anastasia pulled Paulo along and came alongside Esmeralda.

"Did you know you could do that—make that light with your staff?"

"Nope," she said, giggling as if sharing an inside joke. "But let's go with it. It sure is cool!"

"What was that about us having superpowers?"

"Oh, I made that up. We had to get the people to forget about Bob."

"Bob? Really?"

Esmeralda turned to look at the lengthening column of refugees. "Hey, it worked."

"But Ez, I don't *have* any superpowers."

"We don't know that for sure. I mean, turns out I can light up my staff. Maybe you'll find out something about yourself that you didn't know, too."

"I'm fairly certain that I'm pretty ordinary."

"Well, let's hope we don't need to put that to the test, because 'Captain Ordinary' is pretty lame as superhero names go. But you got this far, Sia. That seems pretty extraordinary to me."

She winked and continued on.

Again, they walked for what Anastasia knew had to be hours, yet it was impossible to determine how many. The best way for her to measure progress, at first, was to track the distance between them and the unfinished city of fragments. Its broken off buildings grew smaller against the horizon while the marching line of refugees grew longer. Anastasia kept Paulo close beside her. She felt the first stirrings of hope as he started to remember the hours just before he had been bitten and even began to speak complete sentences. The others around them showed similar signs of recovery, speaking to one another, asking questions, and even remembering the names of loved ones they had left behind.

But looking back behind them at the long column of people, Anastasia noticed something else. They were walking along a ridge. It grew up out of the floor of the wasteland, a long rising spine with steep drops to either side that became nearly sheer as they climbed higher. It was a perilous path. Treacherous gullies and shadowy ravines formed deep fissures, seemingly without bottom, all around them. Anastasia was not sure when they had started up the ridge, but from the long narrow line of refugees stretching along its length, she realized they *had* to have been walking it for long time.

"Esmeralda, is this the way we came?"

"To quote Shakespeare, Hamlet, Act III, Scene 3, Line 87 . . . 'No.'"

"Then what are we doing?"

"The way *in* is always wider than the way *out*," Esmeralda said, looking back over her shoulder, her head surrounded by an aura from her staff.

"All right," Anastasia said. She had learned to just take Esmeralda's word for how things were here in the spirit world. She turned to her brother. "Paulo, do you remember coming to the city?"

"Not really. I just sat up and saw there was nothing else around except those buildings on the horizon. They reminded me of broken teeth. I decided to walk over and look closer. It just seemed to be the thing I should—"

A woman's scream pierced the air. Esmeralda and Anastasia looked up from Paulo to the crowd. Their faces were turned upward in unmistakable horror. Some were beginning to cower. Anastasia spun back around, pushing Paulo behind her, afraid she already knew what they would see.

The shape stood up on the ridge before them, at least twenty meters high. Its features were indistinct in the moving curtains of aether, the red and black panels of his face were muted, but the eye slits of the mask flickered brightly with blue flames. Anastasia knew what, rather *who,* she was looking at: the nameless one, the Devourer of Souls.

She couldn't really bring herself to call him Bob.

With a sound like wood being wrenched to pieces, he opened his mouth to reveal row after row of fangs. As he moved closer, Anastasia could hear his voice, or rather, voices. He spoke not with words but sounds that were broken, like symbols of words, split off and scrambled from their meaning, whispered all at once by many discordant voices. The noise of the chorus was bereft of any purpose save to inspire terror and sow chaos.

He stepped beyond the mists. The bold colors of his face became clear and so did his body, a moving figure of feathery shadows. The darkness of his skin parted in mouth-like slits. Lesser

versions of himself leapt out, lanky figures the size of a Dinka or
Maasai man. They landed upon the ground, one, two, three, followed
by three more. They rushed the crowd, the people surging
backwards, grabbing on to one another to keep from falling off the
edges. Anastasia wrapped her arms around Paulo, afraid he would be
trampled, knocked over the cliffs, or snatched by the demon or his
charging minions.

But before the minions could reach the people, Esmeralda
swept forward, spun her staff, and then did something Anastasia did
not expect.

Esmeralda closed her eyes.

Anastasia was not sure if Esmeralda was sacrificing herself
or drawing the minions to her as a distraction. But the careful,
balanced poise Anastasia was accustomed to seeing in Esmeralda's
posture returned: her back rigid, her free hand out to her side as if to
feel the vibrations of the air. Dirt flew up from the minions' talons.
Her friend's face was calm, placid even, turning her staff now in a
lazy circle, like a windmill in a desultory breeze. That was when
Anastasia realized that this was Esmeralda's battleground of choice;
that she was unafraid to meet the minions in the darkness of her own
terms.

The minions growled and spat gibberish from behind their
masks, their mouths opening with a spray of splinters. Only when
they had closed within a meter did Esmeralda's staff accelerate into
a blur, swinging down and landing with a crack on the first minion's

head. The mask split. A blue light bled out and his shadowy body evaporated, the remnants falling into a smoking pile of ash.

Esmeralda, her eyes still closed, pivoted and struck a second, then a third beast with the same effect. She caught a fourth on the end of her staff and lifted him up overhead, sending him tumbling towards the refugees. Now that they had seen that the minions could be defeated, the grownups among them grabbed rocks and stones from the ridge and smashed a minion's mask. Then they began to rush the others.

A roar came from the Devourer of Souls, and more minions leapt from his body, all screaming like hyenas. Esmeralda continued to spin, thrust, smash, and kill the smaller demons, knocking some over the side while a group of men, feeling confident, rushed the Devourer himself.

It was a grave mistake.

The Devourer stepped forward, his foot landing with a crash that shook the ridge. He swept the men up, one by one, tearing them limb from limb. Their spirit bodies, for what they were, dropped with dull thuds, while their essences scattered in a white mist to mix with the aether.

As quickly as the people had gained confidence, they lost it, cowering once more. Esmeralda dispatched two more minions, landing with her staff tucked under one arm, the other out to the side, her palm turned up like the blade of a knife. Now she opened her eyes to look to Anastasia, who had wrapped Paulo in a protective hug amidst the melee.

"I've got the babies, but I don't know about their daddy, Tinkles," Esmerelda said.

"How close are we to the way out?"

"It's just up there," Esmeralda heaved another minion into the air off the side of the cliff.

Anastasia knew what she had to do. She pulled Paulo close, face to face, "Paulo, whatever happens, you follow Esmeralda. She'll get you home to Mum and Dad. Help the people to follow her."

"What are you going to do?"

"I'm . . . I'm not sure."

"Don't leave!" he said, grabbing hold of her.

"Don't worry, I'll catch up," Anastasia said, peeling his hands away. Paulo let go, his face finally expressive again, even if it was filled with terror.

Once free, Anastasia raced up the slope, dodging a minion as it was blasted into bits. When she tripped and fell, she heard the "WHOOSH" of Esmeralda's staff passing just over her head and the "thud" as it landed a strike against another minion. The beast charged again, but Esmeralda caught it in the eye socket with the end of her staff. She cried out, wrenching the mask out of place, and the minion exploded in a blue flash.

"Thanks, Ez," Anastasia gasped.

"I hope you know what you are doing."

"I do too," Anastasia said, using the opening to pick up a rock as she took to her feet again. The Devourer of Souls was descending closer to the people. Anastasia ran into his field of vision and flung the rock at his face. It struck with the hollow sound of a stone hitting a wooden billboard.

"Hey you, you nameless freak! Yeah you! Over here!" Anastasia bent to pick up another rock and threw it. But this time the nameless thing turned, caught the stone, and crushed it, the dust sprinkling down as the creature turned his glowing eyes to her.

If she had not been in the spirit world, Anastasia was sure that this was when she would feel pee running down her leg.

She had to fight to find her voice and speak over the lump lodged in her throat, "Now that I have your attention . . . you see anything different about me? Yeah, I'm not a zombie or a ghost. I'm a living girl. I bet that sounds appetizing—"

It did. The nameless one rushed her, his face filling up her vision. Anastasia turned to run. Knowing she had his attention, she darted for the path she had picked out moments before, crossing the ridge to a spur of rock and balancing along it. She was starting down the mountainside. It took her onto a narrow and precarious slope with sharp drops to either side. Most importantly, it led away from the crest of the ridge and the people there.

The mountain shook as the Devourer landed with a leap just behind Anastasia, sending dirt and rocks scattering at her back and her feet. He tore up the ground in pursuit. Anastasia risked a quick glance over her shoulder. He was just behind her, but she also saw that Esmeralda had slain the last of the minions, and the people were surging up the ridge to the way out.

Anastasia was too far away to see Paulo clearly. She looked backwards a beat too long, trying to find him in the crush of people. She stumbled, lost her footing, and fell.

The first drop was the longest. Anastasia struck the first ledge with such force that it made her cry out as the air was crushed right out of her lungs. She tumbled further, her arms flung out like a dervish, the world a blur, but among the rocks, the white sky, the dust, and flashes of blood, she caught sight of the Devourer descending after her, barreling down the hillside in an avalanche of pebbles and stones. He was a hunter who had caught the scent of his prey and he was not about to let her slip away.

The slope became less sheer, but still Anastasia tumbled down, bouncing off the hillside, each turn feeling like a punch or a kick, to the face, the gut, wherever. When her momentum had run out and she was weak with the pain of the impacts and sick from the disorientation of such violent spinning, she continued to crawl forward, the noise of the Devourer closing in on her with all the clamor of an earthquake. Her only thought was to lead the nameless thing as far from her brother and all the others as possible. There were copious drops of blood on the ground from her head. Her hands were shredded and raw, the flesh scraped off, leaving bloody prints behind her. Even though she was no longer spinning, her vision was blurred. A ravine, its floor lost in shadow, loomed up to her right. Behind her she could hear the nameless thing, his claws sweeping up the bloody dirt she left behind into his mouth, his fangs crushing the stones that came along with it.

Anastasia rolled closer to the edge, hoping that she might lure him over the side, even if she had to go with him. She kept as close to the edge as possible without falling. The sides were steep and a blanket of aether fog floated in a dense layer. The Devourer moved closer, his cry of many voices like a band of harpies. Anastasia turned to double check how close she was to the edge, but she moved her head too fast. Her inner ear, still disrupted by the previous fall, betrayed her. The world spun anew.

She fell.

More tumbling. More darkness. More cries of the nameless one descending after her. When Anastasia finally landed, the only reason she was not dead—she was sure—was because she was in the spirit realm already. Maybe she was dead, now, and when—if—she returned to the Path, she would be caught in its upward flow, into the afterlife to be with her ancestors, Jesus, or whatever.

The bottom of the ravine was dusty and dark. Anastasia coughed and two blue lights appeared, casting the canyon in a dim glow. The nameless one closed in on her. In addition to the voices without meaning that poured from his gaping maw, she could now hear the flicker of the flames behind his eyes and the rubbing of his blue tongue on the inner sides of his teeth.

Anastasia *wished* she did have some superpower, like Esmeralda had said, but at the moment she knew she was helplessly ordinary. The Devourer's breath was foul, like flesh rotting from gangrene or fungus growing over a grave. It was as hot as sewer gas as well, yet her flesh was still covered in goosebumps, as if a wind blew on her from off a glacier.

Then something Latia had said came to her, and in the strange logic of a dream state, Anastasia put her hand up and said, "Wait . . . wait . . . let me tell you a story."

It was absurd, she knew it. But Latia had talked about the power of story. Dialogue was stronger than chaos, or so Anastasia hoped.

Whatever the case, the nameless one stopped, his giant mask hovering a mere arm's length from Anastasia's face. The wind of his breath, in and out, brushed against her cheeks and moved the ends of her hair.

He was waiting.

"Well, see, uh, let me tell you about how—uh . . ."

The wind of breath grew fierce, impatient. He took a great inhalation, like a carnivore before taking the first bite of its kill.

"—how my friend Latia, she lost her mother and so her father was so sad he sent her away to learn at a school on top of a tree where she became very learned but very lonely, until this one boy Jamhuri . . ."

She spoke quickly, carried now by the momentum of the story Latia had told her before she had fallen asleep, the bedtime story . . . the very incantation that had brought Anastasia to this strange place. But if she hoped the telling of the story would somehow magically wake her and lead her back to the material world, she was disappointed. For as she neared the end, Anastasia did not feel herself drawn back to the waking world in the slightest. Realizing that her remaining life might be measured out in the tales she wove—Arabian Nights style—Anastasia jumped, with little interval, into the next story. And although the Devourer's face loomed just as close as before, those teeth menacing her, the wind of his breath had grown gentle, the voices quiet, as if the lost souls within his bulk were listening. The fire in his eyes burned brighter, but his tongue had gone still. His whole being was listening, bent on her next words as Anastasia unwound the telling of her cousin Njambi's story, her journey through the wilderness, up Mount Kaliande and back. When Anastasia neared the conclusion, having told of how Njambi had returned in the talons of a lammergeyer, she shifted to her own most recent adventure.

"You see, I was just talking to Njambi the other day. She had called because she had heard that my brother had been bitten by a zombie . . . and well, let me tell you, that was *all* my fault."

Anastasia recounted her own story. Her tone was less of a fireside folktale and more like an old friend, speaking to her peer about the course of her day. She led the unnamed one through a reconstruction of the events: how she had ignored her brother, the fight in the garden with the American zombie, her talk with Peter, Njambi, and then her passage through the city to Latia's. If Anastasia didn't know better, she would have thought the Devourer of Souls snorted a small laugh when she mentioned the foolhardy white jogger.

"I know, white people!" she ventured. The joke seemed to land as the nameless one made a grunt of assent. She continued, sharing as best as she could recall, the description of Latia's institute. She sensed that the Devourer of Souls savored the details, so she relayed all she could remember about the different labs, rooms, and artifacts. Anastasia remembered and repeated what she could from her discussion with Latia, although many of the technical details had been lost on her. She brought the story up to her entry into the spirit realm, waking up in the river, meeting Esmeralda, journeying across the wastelands to the city of fragments, and eventually coming to where she was, lying on her side, propped on her elbow, beads of sweat or blood—maybe both—running down the side of her face with the nameless one hovering over her.

"And well, I guess that brings me to . . . uh . . . how we find ourselves here."

Anastasia stopped. Her mouth was dry and her jaw ached. A sharp pain stabbed at her elbow from how she had been leaning on it, but she didn't dare shift her weight, lest she create an opening for the Devourer to . . . well . . . devour her. After the moment of quiet stretched out to a minute, the unnamed one himself shifted, tilting the front of his mask forward even closer. His eyes flared so that Anastasia felt the heat of their rising flames. The whispers grew behind the mask, and for the first time, she understood what they asked.

*How does it end?* The voices were asking.

Anastasia swallowed. She didn't know. All that came to mind was that dumb saying Latia had said about not knowing anything: "Admitting ignorance prepares the soil for the seed of wisdom."

Was honesty the best policy? Anastasia had little left to try.

"I . . . I'm sorry, I don't know."

A scream split her ears, a cracking and groaning of wood as the mouth opened, and the fangs closed on her.

Then nothing.

She floated in a pool of darkness, dwarfed to nothingness by the infinity that surrounded her. But in that infinity, she began to perceive order, filaments of substance in a vacuum. In the filaments floated clusters of light, the froth of waves rippling on a sea of dark matter. And in this froth, were families of spirals, the pinwheel arms of those spirals made of spinning stars orbited by their own halos of jeweled planets, each planet a world with mountains, oceans, caverns within continents. The whims of gods, demons, spirits, and ghosts were the forces that conspired to hold these pieces in unity, collaborating, and sometimes disguised as the quantum and relative forces that held all the elements, big and small, together.

She heard the drip of water again. Not the quick *plink plink plonk* of before, but this time the slow chime of meltwaters dripping, with long intervals in between, each drop finding home in a subterranean pool.

Anastasia opened her eyes.

"She's waking up," a familiar voice said. But Anastasia was not on the phone, nor was she in Kaliande . . .

"Anastasia, can you hear me?"

"Njambi?" she said, blinking, her cousin Njambi's face unexpectedly coming into focus. Njambi was not on Anastasia's phone screen with her room in the background. This time she was right before Anastasia's face. Njambi looked at her, just inches away. She was framed against a backdrop of iridescent ultramarine shot through with veins of silver-white. Her hair was still plaited into cornrows of medium thickness with the wooden beads and cowrie shells that she had worn the last time they had chatted face-to-face on the phone. A necklace with a rainbow array of shiny stones hung around her neck. Its colored stones corresponded to the seven chakras, each separated from one another by contrasting beads made of rough, polished volcanic rock. The necklace rested against a red T-shirt, where a cartoon bunch of protons and neutrons in a cloud of orbiting electrons was set with an expressive cartoon face, his mouth open as if in midsentence. The cartoon atom had legs and arms as well, and he was poised in the animated pose of a storyteller, his arms high above his head, his eyes wide as if he were at the climax of a tall tale. Sans serif letters read out a warning above and below him.

# Don't believe atoms—

# They make up everything.

"Hey, coz."

"Njambi, where am I?"

"An ice cave," Njambi said slowly, as if trying not to shock her, although at this point Anastasia was quite beyond feeling shocked. It did not keep her from commenting on an apparent contradiction she was sensing in the "ice" cave.

"But it feels warm."

"That's because of the pool," Njambi said, offering Anastasia a bowl of water made from the same volcanic stone as the black beads of her necklace. "Drink this. It will help."

Drinking strange substances had brought about some equally strange experiences recently for Anastasia, but this offering from Njambi appeared to be simply water. Anastasia brought the bowl to her lips and drank. As she did, she felt an immediate change, vitality returning to her body. The dull aches and sharp pains all over vanished with a wave of relief. Anastasia was able to sit up and take in the rest of the chamber.

"Njambi, there is a giant bird behind you," Anastasia said, freezing, as a huge yellow and black avian thing stared her down with keen eyes. It looked like a weird mashup of a condor and an eagle wrapped in yellow and black fur instead of feathers.

"Oh, that's just Akinyi. He's a lammergeyer," Njambi said, paying the bird little mind. "He's harmless . . . well, mostly."

As if dissatisfied with only her passing attention, Akinyi leapt up onto Njambi's shoulder, nodding his head and picking at the space between her cornrows. She tweaked his beak back. "Stop it. Be a good boy and go tell Ife that Anastasia is awake."

The lammergeyer squawked, flapped his wings, and was away in a rush of air, not unlike the first stirrings of a storm.

"Njambi, am I dead?"

"No, no, you are alive."

"Where am I then, exactly?"

"Well, that is harder to say, *exactly*. You're still technically in Dr. Solei's office in the capital."

Anastasia looked around at the cave, then back at herself. Her arms, legs, hands, torso looked real enough. "But I'm here . . . am I a ghost?"

"No, you are a *sending*. A manifestation of your body. You'd be like a ghost, transparent, if you stepped outside this cave, but inside here things are . . . different. You'll feel as real here as if you were in the material world."

"Are you . . . here, for real?" Anastasia said, clutching her cousin's hand.

"Yes," Njambi smiled, amused and compassionate at once.

Anastasia looked around again, taking in the pool, the ice that glowed above it with light from some unseen source. The ground was stone but warm. So was the wall behind her. Anastasia jumped, startled, when she saw what was painted on its surface.

"It's him!" she said, moving close to Njambi.

"It's just a painting, I think. But he's nothing to be afraid of," Njambi said, while they both regarded the red-black visage, the fierce blue eyes with black irises, and the gleaming white fangs of the nameless one. The painting loomed close, as if to devour Anastasia once more. "You met him?" Njambi asked, curious.

"Uh yeah, you could say that," Anastasia said, touching her forehead. The wounds were gone. "Njambi, what the heck is happening?"

"Better she explains," her cousin replied, nodding for Anastasia to look back in the direction of the pool. Anastasia braced for something terrible. But in this case, she was relieved. A woman was walking over to them. She was statuesque, regal and beautiful. Her skin was a dark ebony, and the curves of her figure were hugged by a wrap of burgundy with blue patterns throughout. Black and white bangles decorated her arms, and a leather choker held a sapphire over her throat like a blue star.

She was *walking* across the pool—Jesus like—rings of ripples spreading out from where her feet touched the surface of the water. "Welcome, Anastasia. I am Ife."

Anastasia bowed her head. Everything about the woman's appearance bespoke that she was someone, some*thing*, more than she appeared. Akinyi the lammergeyer flapped back into place next to Njambi, and she fed him a few seeds she pulled from her pocket.

"Tell me, Anastasia, what do you remember?" Ife asked, still standing miraculously on the surface of the water. Njambi, for her part, was unperturbed by this, as if it was natural and normal that mysterious, beautiful women hung out in ice caves and walked on water all the time.

"I just remember that thing," Anastasia said, tipping her head to the wall but stopping short of looking into the face of the Devourer again. She did not want to meet the eyes of the demon or turn her back to this woman whom she was certain was a goddess of some type. "I thought I was dead."

"A fair conclusion, as the nameless one is the source of death, destruction, and chaos."

"But then why am I here. Is everyone safe? Paulo, Esmeralda, the others?"

"They are all on their way home, each and everyone one of them," Ife said. Anastasia could have wept with joy and relief. It didn't occur to her to ask if she would be joining them; she assumed she would find out where she was headed soon enough. Perhaps this cave was just a stopping point on the way to the afterlife, and Njambi's reassurances that she was not dead needed to be qualified by a "yet." On reflection, Anastasia realized, she was at peace with such an outcome. It was enough that Paulo, Esmeralda, and the refugees were safe.

"You all right, Sia?"

"Yeah, more than all right," she said, wiping some tears and repeating herself, "More than all right."

She took a few moments to compose herself, Akinyi even moving in close to tap Anastasia gently on the head with his beak, as if in reassurance. She found herself petting the bird, his feathers as soft as fur on a cat's neck. "I just don't know what happened. I'm so confused."

"I was too. I still am. You learn to get used to it," Njambi said.

"Perhaps I can help," Ife offered, her lips curving into a smile.

"Yes, of course my lady," Anastasia said.

"You've been a wise and courageous young woman, showing heart, quick wits, and selflessness. In short, Anastasia, you have grown."

"Thank you, my lady," Anastasia said, although she wasn't sure how much she had grown. The choices she had made felt less like choices than imperatives—there had been little choice at all when faced with the peril of her loved ones.

"The balance of things has been disturbed and still has not yet been put back into its rightful place—completely. But the greatest part of the work has been done by releasing the ghosts of the zombies from Limbo. The outbreak will end, but the original wound has yet to be healed. The fabric of the cosmos still bleeds." Ife paused. A drip of water chimed into the pool; her eyes darted to the spreading ripples. "The task of that healing will also fall to you, Anastasia."

Anastasia stiffened. Njambi rubbed her back. "It will be fine. You can handle it."

"Is it him, my lady?" Anastasia asked, inclining her head at the cave painting but still not looking at the unnamed one. "Is he tearing things apart? Can't you destroy him?"

Ife's lips parted in a kind smile that displayed her own bright, white teeth. "I would not destroy him any sooner than I would destroy myself. He *is* me."

Anastasia was confused again. Njambi read it on her face. "I know, I know, just roll with it. Just listen," her cousin said.

Ife continued, "He is the other side of me. While I can sustain life, growing it and nurturing it, I cannot create it. *He* is the life spark that sets the universe in motion. And with the power to create life, comes the power to end it too. One requires the other. I bring things together, he shakes them up. I am order. He is chaos. I am the garden; he is the gardener. Without both of us, there would be no life, no death, no movement—only stasis."

Anastasia looked over to Njambi again, who shrugged. "They like to speak in metaphors. It's a little hard to follow, but it's the best you'll get. They're gods after all . . . completely transcendent. If we totally understood them—well, we can't. 'Cause our heads would explode."

"Literally?"

"Pretty much."

Anastasia would take metaphors over her head exploding any day.

Ife had crossed the water, stepped onto the ground, and settled down next to the two of them, casual like, just chillin', a goddess with two girls, one real, one a sending—whatever *that* was.

*Roll with it. Totally normal,* Anastasia tried to tell herself.

"Your guide Latia has learned much, and she has taught you well in a short time. You managed to succeed despite great odds," Ife said.

Anastasia knew praise when she heard it and thanked Ife again.

"Your time here grows short and like I said, you have one task left to accomplish before all is set right, so listen to my next words with care . . ."

Latia shifted the Land Rover into neutral, the engine idling as the country's seal stared back at them from the gate of the presidential residence.

"You sure about his?" Latia asked, looking across the armrest at Anastasia. Dr. Solei had believed everything Anastasia had shared about her otherworldly experience, soaking up every nuance and detail with fevered writing in her notebook. She had mostly refrained from interrupting, so as not to disrupt Anastasia's flow, although Anastasia had seen her jot down more than a dozen questions, which Latia said they would "bookmark for later."

Anastasia knew Latia's hesitation now stemmed from a concern for their safety and not from any doubts about her story. Anastasia had survived her quest through the spirit world, but trespassing in the presidential residence could carry dangers and consequences in the material world that neither of them would be safe from. Prison time would be the best-case scenario, if they were not shot on sight, having been mistaken for assassins, looters, political insurgents, or all three.

But Anastasia had a hunch they just might get away with their plan. There was no sign of any guards at the gate. Likely they had abandoned their post to go protect their own families. After all, the zombies were still about. Ife had said that the ghosts were on their way back. Anastasia had no reason to doubt her, but she also knew that time moved differently in the spirit world than the material one.

"Look, the gate isn't even locked," Anastasia said, pointing to a gap between the doors. She put her hand on the Rover's door handle to get out. "I'll open it."

"Careful," Latia said. Anastasia could tell Latia didn't like the idea of her getting out of the vehicle, but Anastasia couldn't drive, the intricacies of the gearshift, the clutch, and friction points all still elusive to her. So she got out, climbed down to the ground, and crept up on the gate. It was strange to see the country's seal so close, with its gold and black lammergeyer (much like Akinyi) spread against the backdrop of snowy volcanoes and sun-kissed savanna. How many times had she seen this very gate as a backdrop while journalists relayed their stories on the evening news, reporting on another accomplishment of the Wukumbo Presidential Administration: reducing malaria or maternal/child mortality; supporting economic growth, achievements in education, or grants to the arts. Their country had been the crown jewel of African countries, praised all around the world.

Until now.

Now the seal, that symbol of their country's autonomy, solidarity, and independence, was mute, abandoned, and literally split down the center, one half moving to either side of the gate as Anastasia pushed the doors open. They swung inward without resistance or alarm, revealing an expanse of lawn that was empty but for a few colobus monkeys that scattered back up into the trees at the sound of Latia revving the Rover's engine and rolling inside. By the look on Latia's face, Anastasia knew she wanted her back in the car.

Anastasia climbed inside and locked her door. Latia drove them up the long driveway in silence, both of them scanning the grounds for any signs of soldiers, bodyguards, police, or zombies. There were none. When they rolled up to the portico where the presidential motorcade usually would park, they found no one: not a driver, a groundskeeper, or even a maid.

They got out, closing the doors without slamming them, and went inside.

They were in the presidential residence. There was no going back now. It felt like the worst of possible trespasses. Everything reminded them that they did not belong: the red carpet, the gilded chandeliers, the art installations donated by artists from all over the continent. French doors separated one grand room from the next. The residence struck Anastasia as more like a museum than a home. She couldn't imagine feeling "comfortable" in such a space. It was stuffy, formal, and smelled of chemical cleaners.

They moved slowly down the hallway, then the next, exploring staterooms, pressrooms, dining rooms, trying to announce themselves with tentative "hellos." Latia, for all her training and accomplishments, wore a face of meekness, her head a little bowed, like a child trespassing in her parents' study. It was Anastasia who led them now. They reached the office of the president herself. It appeared a little more lived-in, with loose papers scattered on the desk and the coffee table. Latia gravitated to the desk. A laptop was docked in the docking port. Two flat-screen displays had windows open to a half a dozen news sites. Videos of reporters providing stories from within the country as well as outside it were playing, the sound muted on all of them.

Anastasia was drawn to a side door that led to an adjacent study. The door was ajar. She moved to tap on it; the knocking itself was enough to send it swinging open.

She sucked in her breath when she saw the other side. It was a room lined with books from floor to ceiling, reminiscent of Latia's study. It was lit by skylights. Ceiling fans hummed overhead, rustling the pages of a series of thick, ancient tomes left open on a coffee table. Seated in front of them, her eyes red from tears or insomnia, her face sad and drawn, as if she had not eaten in many days, was President Ajuma Wukumbo herself.

The president wore a simple white dress with a black sash over her shoulders and a plain leather belt without beads, tassels, or other adornment. She was in her fifties and had always appeared youthful on television, standing with a supreme confidence, her shoulders set, her back arched, a hand always ready to wave while she flashed her famous smile.

But the woman before them was changed. Anastasia might not have even recognized her as the president had they met on the street. Her shoulders were pinched, her head bowed. She showed no surprise or anger at their trespass; rather, she appeared lost under a burden of grief, staring at her empty hands, resting upturned on her knees. The light from the skylights had shifted so that it no longer fell on her but, instead, on the pages of the books before her. The president herself was cast in shadow. There was no telling how long she had sat there, but Anastasia sensed it had been for a long time.

"Madam President," Anastasia curtseyed. Latia moved up behind her, gasped, and did the same.

President Wukumbo studied them with those eyes that had looked over multitudes, eyes that had seen a vision for their country. She took in the young women who had penetrated the perimeter to reach her innermost sanctum, before turning her face back to the floor.

"I am no president. A president has a country."

She said nothing more, her face empty of anything, save pain and regret. It reminded Anastasia of the faces of the ghosts when they had still been in the city of fragments, instruments reduced to just one note.

"Madam President . . ." Latia said, but her voice trailed off.

"Is there anything left?"

"Madam?" Anastasia asked.

"Of our country. The country I ruined."

"Madam President, you—" Anastasia stopped. Latia placed her hand on her shoulder, a signal to be quiet and listen. The president covered her face with her hands and began to weep.

It was striking for Anastasia, to see such a powerful, invincible woman so vulnerable, so wounded.

*So human.*

"It is all my fault."

Latia and Anastasia both seemed to forget that this was the president, responding to her more as a grieving human. They moved around the coffee table and sat on the couch to either side of her. Anastasia noticed Latia adjust her glasses and take in the open books. They were in a variety of languages, with different symbols and signs. Anastasia recognized what she thought were Adinkra symbols, Swahili, Arabic, Hieroglyphics, Hebrew, Amharic, Persian, Pashtun, Hindi, ancient Greek, Latin, even ancient Sumerian.

*So many languages.*

Alongside the books were crucibles, mortars, and pestles. Small flasks of dark inky liquids rested alongside vials of milky ones. There was also a digital scale and thermometer and a number of articles printed out from medical and science journals, their corners stapled, their paragraphs highlighted and underlined with copious notes and formulas scribbled in the margins. Anastasia recognized this mix of science and magic by now, much like what she had seen in Latia's institute.

That meant the president also knew magic. . .

"You all think you know who your president is. Everyone does. But they are wrong. I am an imposter."

"Madam, you are our president," Latia reassured her. "Our leader."

"I have only led us to ruin. Yes, I am a leader, a role I play like mother, widow, daughter, and sister. It is that last one, *sister,* which is the source of my greatest failure and greatest shame. I tried to bury that secret in the dark, but darkness and lies, they have a way of coming to light. They spread their poison to everything else. All this—" she said with a sweep of her arm at the table and its array of ancient and modern wisdom, "—this was my attempt to fix that. But I overreached. I brought ruin upon us, upon so many innocents who did not deserve such suffering."

Latia leaned closer to the table, putting on her scholar's gaze again. She picked up an article, skimmed the title and the abstract before putting it down and consulting some of the older books, reading some of the chapter titles aloud. "Prima Materia and the Philosopher's Stone, Coptic Alchemy, The Waters of Bimini, Time Dilation in the Mahabharata, Formula for the Waters of Lethe,

Diagrams of an Einstein-Rosen Bridge . . . spells of reversal, healing, forgetfulness, theories on time travel. Madam President, what were you trying to change?"

"The past, to erase my mistakes. I know, it was arrogant, outrageous, but understand, I was trying to fix my greatest hurt and worst betrayal. But all I succeeded in doing was splitting the souls from our peoples' bodies, cursing them with forgetfulness. I've tried to repair, but it only made things worse."

The president's voice was weary, full of defeat. Empathy twisted Anastasia's stomach, for she too was familiar with the desire to repair mistakes. She wanted to tell the president of her own meetings with gods and spirits in the preceding hours—had it only been hours? It felt like days, weeks even—but Latia's eyes still sent the clear message that it was not the time to talk, but rather, to listen.

And the president shared her story.

"I was just a girl—popular and smart, yes, but not wise, and very selfish and vain. You see, my little brother was ill with malaria. I was supposed to remain home watching him, making sure he took his medicine every two hours. But I wanted to go out with my friends. My parents were out for the day working. They had to be. We were poor. So I gave my brother two doses at once to cover him for four hours so I could sneak out. I had a life to live, after all, and it was not *my* fault he was sick.

"I left him sleeping, went out, and came back right on time, satisfied with myself and how I had met my family and social obligations, even outsmarting my dumb parents while doing it. I thought all was well. But it wasn't. You see, malaria medicines were not as safe back then." She turned to Latia, who still wore her lab coat, and touched her knee. "You know, I'm sure. There were always dangerous side effects that a stupid, selfish, teenage girl would not have thought of." A few more jagged sobs shook President Wukumbo's frame. She wiped her eyes and nose. "My brother was *blinded.* All because of me. I was supposed to protect him, to care for him, but I betrayed him. I let down my parents. He had such a kind heart, always taking in little animals and nursing them back to health. He could coax anything to grow, to flourish, including plants. He had a green thumb. My parents, they had such high hopes for him. He was talented with drawing, painting, and sculpting. We hoped he might grow up to be an artist, but I took all that away from him.

"And me. I was supposed to be the smart daughter, responsible, respectable. I had become their worst failure. I was so ashamed that I ran away. I lived on the streets. I survived because other poor children and women, who had so little to give, took me in out of sympathy. I told them I was an orphan. I changed my name and worked odd jobs. A group of women who owned some local businesses in the slums started to look after me. They saw potential in me and paid for my schooling. I learned important lessons in those years. It gave me a heart for the indigent, but also an understanding of how women could come together and lift themselves up through business. I was determined to give back, and I did. It led me here. I was so driven, so committed, so passionate. I wanted to take care of the whole country."

"And you have," Latia said. "People say you are the greatest president the country has ever seen, even the whole continent."

"But you see," said President Wukumbo, turning to Latia, twisting the end of her sash in her hands. "I couldn't care for the one person who needed me most. Now I have tried too hard and spread my failure to everyone. I am cursed and the country, too."

She covered her face once more. Latia was overwhelmed, her own eyes filming. She put her arm around the president and rubbed her back, as she might a sister. They clasped hands. Anastasia, risking being too forward herself, reached out for the president's other hand. "Madam president, I think I would like to take you someplace with us."

Anastasia rode in the backseat with President Wukumbo while Latia drove them. It was a measure of her despair that the president accompanied them without question. Anastasia guessed that President Wukumbo was grateful to hand over responsibility to someone else, to be led instead of leading, even if she had only just met them. She apparently had no one else, having sent her own staff away, like Latia had, to care for their families. It was clear the president trusted the two of them. With the disaster that had befallen the country, normal social barriers had broken down.

So that was how a twenty-something doctor from a village in the Southern Region and a teenage girl found themselves driving the president of the most powerful African country up to the gate of Anastasia's house—Anastasia whispering a prayer under her breath that her plan would work.

Latia honked the horn outside the locked gate. When Anastasia saw her father open the guard latch and peer through at the stranger in an unfamiliar vehicle with "Saitoti Research Institute" written on the door, Anastasia realized he would likely think they were from the Ministry of Health, come to quarantine them. She rolled down the window.

"Papa, it's me!"

"Anastasia!"

He ran to open the gate without closing the latch. Latia shifted into gear and the Rover roared into the courtyard. Her father was calling out at the windows to her grandmother, mother, and aunts. "Lizabeth, Beatrice, Kadija, and Kamaria—come quick, Anastasia has come home!"

Anastasia opened the door. She wasn't sure if she should expect a beating or a hug, but she got out of the car anyway. To her relief, her father knelt down and wrapped her in a tight embrace.

"I thought I would lose both my children."

Her father was weeping, something she had never seen him do before.

"Papa, I'm so sorry."

A series of quick taps of her cane preceded Esmeralda running in from the lane between the house and the wall to the next compound.

"Esmeralda!" Anastasia said, leaping to her. The young woman, to her surprise, hugged her even tighter than her father. She was smiling and laughing.

"I knew you would return!"

"Esmeralda, you were magnificent," Anastasia said, pulling back just enough to see her friend's face. Esmeralda ran her fingers lightly across Anastasia's cheeks, eyes, and mouth, reading her happiness with her touch. Anastasia reached up to touch Esmeralda's face as well, at first in affection, but then she closed her eyes as well. "You'll have to teach me to *see* like you do."

Esmeralda punched her arm. "All right, I guess I can show you some of my moves. You need something other than throwing rocks."

They both laughed. "You're right about that."

"I'll have to blindfold you to do it proper."

"I'm in."

Anastasia's grandmother, Lizabeth, and her aunties Beatrice and Kadija ran into the courtyard next, crushing Anastasia in more hugs. They were less restrained with their weeping than her father had been, but swiftly shifting to jumping and singing praises to Jesus, God, and the ancestors for her safe return. Anastasia tried to give them a moment to savor their relief before she asked, "How is Paulo?"

The joy on their faces faded. "The same," Grandma Lizabeth said.

"Worse really," Aunt Beatrice said, Aunt Kadija nodding her head with a somber look.

"And Mum?"

"Kamaria is with him. She had dozed off next to his bed."

Two car doors closed drawing Anastasia's attention back to the Rover. Already all the adults had gone silent at the sight of the president. After the initial shock, Grandma Lizabeth, being of an older generation, pulled her shawl over her head and knelt before President Wukumbo, just as her elders had done for chiefs—bad knees and all. Her aunties looked completely befuddled and stunned, placing their hands over their hearts before they simply followed Grandma Lizabeth's example, as none of them had ever met a president before.

Her father was unsure whether to bow or kneel or to greet her with a handshake and welcome her as the host. He stumbled over his words, looking back and forth between the president and Latia, as if she were some aide who might explain the official protocol. Anastasia realized that even careworn, brokenhearted, and tired, President Wukumbo still retained a regal air, whether she felt it or not. It was Anastasia, in the end, who spoke up to announce the president.

"Uh, Dad, Aunties, Grandmama, Esmeralda, please meet my friends, Dr. Latia Solei and President Wukumbo."

"President Wukumbo, here? Where? Is that why everyone is acting so weird all the sudden?" Esmeralda asked.

"Yeah, she just got out of the Rover I came in. I'll explain—"

Before she could finish, Anastasia heard the sound she had been waiting for: the *tip, tap, tip* of Peter coming down the lane Esmeralda had emerged from. Anastasia ran to meet him, taking his hands as he emerged into the courtyard. "Motinda!"

"My little Starflower, I knew you would return."

"I have. I . . . I listened to your story, Motinda. I tried to learn from it. I think . . . I think I found out how it ends."

"You did?"

"Yes." Anastasia turned, but already the president had closed the distance between them, her hands to her mouth.

"Peter . . . Peter Motinda?"

Peter froze, his back stiffening. "Well, hello ma'am, I am afraid I am at a bit of a disadvantage . . . have we met? I must say, your voice sounds so much like President Wukumbo."

"That is because she *is* President Wukumbo," Anastasia said.

But the president rushed to take Peter's hands and pressed them to her face, which was wet with tears. "Peter, oh Peter, it's me, it's your sister, Tamaret. I know it's been so long. I am so sorry. . ."

"Tamaret . . . my sister. . ."

"Yes."

Peter traced the bones that gave structure to President Wukumbo's face: her cheeks, her mouth, her nose, the ridge of her brow, the shape of her eyes. She remained still, as if used to his touch from a previous lifetime. After a moment, Peter cried out, "Tamaret!"

They both embraced. President Wukumbo—*Tamaret*—blubbering a long overdue apology: "Peter, Motinda, I was so ashamed. I ran away, but I never forgot you. I . . . I tried to make up for it. I tried to take care of others, because I was so ashamed that I had not taken care of you."

"Shhhh," Peter soothed her. "My sister has returned to me." He moved back, touching her face again and the curl of her smile and her falling tears. "And she is the *president*. My sister! I am so proud!"

Anastasia heard Latia sniff. Her aunties and grandmother were wiping their eyes too. Esmeralda was beaming, but still no one spoke, as the moment felt sacred for the reunited brother and sister. At least until a small groggy voice, slurred as if just waking up, broke the silence.

"Grandmama, Auntie, Papa . . . what's going on?"

"Paulo!"

They all turned and rushed the doorway where Paulo was standing, leaning against the doorjamb and rubbing sleep out of his eyes. He swayed, unsteady on his feet, but his skin had returned to its normal color. He had removed the bandages from his shoulder.

His wound had healed, and although everyone moved at once towards him, it was Anastasia who reached him first.

"Ewww, Sia, stop kissing me! Why is everyone acting so weird?"

"That was what I said!" Esmeralda echoed.

Grandma Lizabeth and their aunties began to sing again; even her father joined them this time. All at once, other voices rose up, joining them from all around the neighborhood. Car horns began to honk. Neighbors were banging cooking pots all around, crying out, "The plague is over! The plague is over!"

It was Latia who attempted to explain. "It was your reunion, Madam President and Mr. Motinda. That was the final key to break the curse."

"I don't understand," Peter said.

"It was me, Motinda," his sister, President Wukumbo—Tamaret—said. "I tampered with powers I should not have, trying to undo what I had done to you all those years ago."

"My sister, you are so kind, but forgive yourself. I have. Our scars heal and reveal us and who we are truly meant to be."

"Madam President, if it were not for Peter, I would never have learned to live without my ability to see," Esmeralda said, coming alongside them.

"And if it weren't for Esmeralda, none of the ghosts would have found their way home from Limbo," Anastasia added.

"Ghosts, Limbo, what is all this you are talking about?" Anastasia's father asked.

Their answer was interrupted by Anastasia and Paulo's mother. Kamaria, roused by the noises of celebration, had awoken to find Paulo gone and come running downstairs. Her face showed that she had suspected the worst—that the change had taken place. But seeing Anastasia and Paulo, she stood shocked.

"I am dreaming?"

"No Mum, you're not."

She embraced both her children. It was Anastasia's turn to cry as she tried to apologize, but all her mother would say was, "Shhhh, I love you, I love you, I love you, my sweets. Nothing either of you could do could make me love you any less."

While Paulo, Anastasia, and their mother held one another, it was Latia who suggested they go inside.

"We should all sit down for some tea, if I can be so presumptuous. We have some stories to tell, and you all will want to be sitting down when you hear them."

It was the first of many teas with President Wukumbo, Peter, Latia, Esmeralda and Anastasia's reunited family. After a few weeks of the country recovering and rebuilding from the zombie scourge, Anastasia's parents hosted a garden celebration. The president herself attended, sitting next to her brother Peter just like any other guest (just one with bodyguards and a small army of assistants). She brought her grown children and their children as well, to meet their long-lost uncle. The neighbors were invited too, mingling with the dignitaries, ministers, and ambassadors. Anastasia's parents allowed a few reporters but no cameras. The ambassador from the United States was there, along with Stewart—the American tourist who had been turned into a zombie boy and had bit her brother—and his parents. Anastasia was relieved to see that Stewart had traded in the safari gear for jeans, a T-shirt, and a baseball cap. She was even standing close enough to hear the first awkward exchange between Paulo and Stewart, since they both had been changed back.

"Thanks for inviting us . . . it's really nice of you . . . you know, uh, considering everything," Stewart said.

"Well, my father insists there is a place at our table for everyone. And after all, your parents went through the same fright mine did."

"Yeah, I guess," Stewart said, adjusting the bill of his cap. "Well, I'm still sorry—for trying to eat your flesh and all."

Paulo, always sweet, patted him on the back. "You couldn't help it, and I guess it could have turned out a lot worse."

"Yeah."

They shared an awkward silence, her brother rocking on his heels and Stewart looking up as if to count all the Chinese lanterns strung across the garden. A highlife band was playing down on the lowest terrace, about where Anastasia had come across Stewart and her brother in the first place.

"You want to try some good African food?" Paulo finally said.

"Sure, but no meat. I'm going vegetarian, for obvious reasons."

Anastasia was glad to see them both walk away laughing.

Njambi sidled up next to Anastasia with a Stoney Tangawizi in her hand and handed a freshly opened bottle to Anastasia. Njambi's cornrows were oiled, and her eyes sparkled with glitter. She was wearing a navy blue shirt that read in large red and white characters:

$$\sqrt{-1} \ 2^3 \ \Sigma \ \pi \ \&$$

## It was delicious.

"You really go all-in on those shirts," Anastasia said, after deciphering its meaning.

"Go big or go home," Njambi said, sipping the Tangawizi and coughing right after from the powerful dose of ginger. "Your friends Alba and Winnie are so cool."

"Yeah, they are."

"But your friend James, is he always that annoying?"

"That just means he likes you."

"Ugh, really?"

"He's not so bad, when he's not chewing gum."

Akinyi, who had accompanied Njambi from Kaliande, swooped down from one of the lines of Chinese lanterns to snatch a few morsels of food from the table.

"Hey, your lemminggrabber is stealing food."

"Lammergeyer"

"Whatever."

"Are you going to stop him?"

"No, but she will."

Akinyi swooped down a second time, only to be knocked aside with a loud "THWACK" from Esmeralda's staff. The lammergeyer fluttered clumsily in a cloud of feathers to land on a bush, as surprised as they were. Esmeralda drew her staff close once more and crossed her arms. The giant bird squawked at Esmeralda, but he made no move whatsoever to go near the table again.

"How does she do that?"

"I'm still learning," Anastasia said.

"She's amazing."

"I know." Anastasia sipped her Tangawizi, coughed herself, taking in the crowd of family and friends, old and new. She pictured the long column of refugees snaking its way out of the city of fragments, up the ridge, and imagined many of them celebrating with their own families, or their ancestors in the next life, or whatever destinations their faith had bound them for. As she had learned from Latia, the universe was full of possibilities, and they all could somehow exist at once. No matter where the souls had gone, Anastasia could feel their appreciation and approval, almost like she could sense the direction of the sun with her eyes closed, just by the warmth on her face.

She was glad they had found the ends of their stories.

"Too bad your friend Dr. Solei couldn't make it. I really wanted to meet her," Njambi said.

"Yeah, I wanted you to meet Latia too. But she had something important come up."

"Something at the institute?"

Anastasia smiled. "Something better. She went home to her village in the Southern Region. She said she had a date with her old friend Jamhuri Jumari. I told her she should definitely go. They have a lot of catching up to do."

# ~ Special Thanks ~

To Snorg Tees (snorgtees.com) for the awesome T-shirt ideas. To Emily Esfahani Smith, whose TED Talk introduced me to the term "redemptive story," and my father, who shared the concept behind it when I was young. To Anne Fadiman, whose imagery about the thread of "story" connecting to universal themes has stuck with me since hearing her speak in North Carolina in 2008. To Agata Broncel at Bukovero Designs, who continues to blow my mind with her artistry and book cover designs. To Thomas Merton, James Baldwin, Richard Rohr, Richard Dahlstrom, and Prentice Park, for their faith, thoughts, and philosophies, shared in writings, reflection, and sermons. To Hank Green, whose Crash Course Philosophy series introduced me to the conundrum that got the last section of this novella going: "What are the implications of living in a world where you could be a zombie and a ghost?" And finally, to the Gremlins, who asked me to "tell a story" before bedtime, all those years ago.

## ～ Back Page Matters ～

Thanks so much for reading. If you enjoyed this book and would like to know about giveaways and/or when new books by Ted Neill are available, please send an email to TENEBRAYPRESS@YAHOO.COM with the subject ADD TO MAILING LIST, or visit TENEBRAYPRESS.COM. This comes with a promise NOT to flood your inbox with superfluous messages.

If you want to know more about the children who helped to inspire these stories, take a look at the author's memoir, *Two Years of Wonder,* about his time living at Rainbow Children's Home. All proceeds from *Two Years of Wonder* go back to the children who are featured in its pages and who inspired this book as well.

Finally, your honest reviews wherever books are sold or discussed online ***really matter.*** They help bring credibility to independently published writers like myself and provide potential readers with information that helps them discover new books. Always a plus!

*"When I have a little money, I buy books; and if I have any left, I buy food and clothes."*

*–Erasmus*

# ~ Please Consider Supporting ~

These organizations are all ones the author knows well. They lift up the kind of children who inspired *Jamhuri, Njambi & Fighting Zombies.* Your support is appreciated.

## GrassROOTS & 1000 Black Girl Books

https://grassrootscommunityfoundation.org/

GrassROOTS Community Foundation (GCF) is a public health and social action organization that invests in community members' collective well-being, so that they can use their health and energy to transform themselves, their families and communities. GCF supports, develops and scales health and wellness programs for women and girls, particularly those who are impoverished. They also advocate for policies and practices that foster equity and reduce disparities. They are a proud collaborator with **#1000BlackGirlBooks,** an initiative started by Marley Dias when she was in *sixth grade* to promote books in which black girls are the main characters. https://grassrootscommunityfoundation.org/1000-black-girl-books-resource-guide/

## Little Rock ECD Center

http://littlerockkenya.org/newsite/

Little Rock is situated close to the heart of Nairobi, Kenya. Little Rock was founded by Lilly Oyare in response to the lack of services and community supporting children living with a range of disabilities such as cerebral palsy, visual/hearing impairment, developmental delays, or other special needs. Little Rock mainstreams special needs children alongside normal learners, helping to erase stigma as well as creating an inclusive community that benefits all. Little Rock provides professional development training for teachers in special education as well as numerous emotional and educational supports to parents.

## Harlem Children's Zone

https://hcz.org/

HCZ's mission is to give kids the individualized support they need to get *to and through* college and become productive, self-sustaining adults. This goal is difficult and complex, so HCZ begins work at birth and helps kids every step of the way until college graduation. They accomplish this through a holistic focus on exceptional education, social services, family support, health, and community-building programs. HCZ uses data to constantly evolve and improve, creating inspirational success stories that are shining examples of what can be done when science and compassion are brought together for measurable results and lasting impact.

Made in the USA
San Bernardino, CA
03 December 2018